THE
DRAGON'S DAUGHTER

BY
CLYDE C. WESTOVER

Author of "The Romance of Gentle Will,"
and other stories

Published by Left of Brain Books

ISBN 978-1-396-32156-6

First Edition

Table of Contents

CHAPTER I

CELESTIAL CUNNING

Louie Toy, musing in the doorway of the Canton Bazaar, was awakened from a brocaded dream of Cathay by the sharp crack of a revolver and, as his slanting eyes widened, a slight figure darted around the corner of Clay street and, after a hesitant glance at the Chinaman, stumbled over his threshold and leaned, breathing brokenly, against a glass show-case.

"Madre Dios," he panted, "they will kill!"

Louie Toy turned, stood for a moment, and something stirred within him, something which the Celestial could not analyze.

The figure was so pitiful, so diminutive, so broken. A Mexican, scarcely more than a boy, olive-skinned face streaked with dirt, eyes, long lashed eyes, rolling appealingly, an almost Oriental cast of features. Behind the impassive countenance of the Chinaman that intangible something mastered his brain and, as a clamor of shouts and pattering footsteps sounded on the pavement, he called sharply, "Fong Toon!" and the face of another Mongolian peered through a beaded portière at the rear of the store.

"Mujercita mea!" sobbed the Mexican, "I struck, and they will kill." His fingers clutched the edge of the case, his knees sagged under him, and the voices outside swelled into an angry chorus. A loud cry, distinguishable above the rest, decided Louie Toy and caused him to frown menacingly.

"The White Devil," he muttered in Chinese. "Quick, Fong Toon. Hide this *Tsai* below the stairs!"

His clerk threw an arm around the frightened creature's waist, half dragged, half carried him past the ebony and gold Cashier's window and into the shadow of soft Oriental hangings, while Louie, hands thrust deep into his capacious sleeves, swung about and leaned sleepily against the jamb of the door as a blue-coated policeman, heading a crowd of tenderloin toughs and carrying an automatic revolver in his hand, stopped at the entrance, with an arrogant query.

"Hello, *pung yow*, where the hell's that greaser?"

Louie Toy yawned, wriggled lazily as his eyes widened, and smiled the vacuous smile of serene indifference.

"What's malla, Offici Mulcahey? You chasem tief to-day?"

"Aw, cut it out, Louie!" snapped the policeman. "Lucero knifed his girl, and I think I winged him. He went up that hill like a scared rabbit. Which way did he go?"

Louie Toy's interest seemed to awaken.

"Lilla Mexican boy?" he drawled.

"Yes, yes!"

"Don't know," with a yawn.

"Hell," snapped Mulcahey, "you saw him." "Which way? Come out of your trance!"

Louie blinked. "Him lun up Dupont, down Saclamento; you no like stop dlinkee tea?"

But his last words were spoken to empty ears, for the copper, with an oath, dashed up the block, and Louie smiled inscrutably as the last pair of clattering heels vanished around the corner in a vain race down Sacramento street hill.

"Dog," he muttered, "white dog! He spoils my traffic in *ah-peen-yeen*.[1] Louie Toy, whose ancestor was the great Ho Mun, under the rule of an Irish policeman!"

The indolent look in his eyes gave way to a gleam of malevolence as he shuffled into his doorway, calling softly: "Sen Chee! Sen Chee!!"

Soft-sandaled feet pattered on a little half-balcony at the back of the store, there was a swish of silken hangings, and a pretty Chinese miss, about eighteen years old, minced down the stairway and met her father with a low, gurgling cry of pleasure.

Her black hair was coiled on top of her head and drooped loosely about her temples, curling above her brows, dressed unlike the usual oily coiffure of the Chinese woman, which is drawn in unguent sleekness straight back from the ears, but straying roguishly after the manner affected by her American sisters. Her loose-fitting jacket, rose-colored, and trousers of jade-green, heavily brocaded, looked not at all ugly on her lithe figure; and her dainty,

---

[1] Opium.

embroidered slippers were so tiny that she seemed a quaint Oriental doll, doll-shod and doll-garbed, with a slight rose tinge in olive cheeks, brows pencil-arched in a thin black line, and lashes that drooped over timid eyes.

There was a thrill of affection in Louie's voice.

"My little Lily Flower, my Sen Chee, were you frightened? The White Pig matched his cunning against that of Louie Toy. He has many five tael tins of the precious drug to his account. He will pay. He will pay!" He smiled again upon the girl. "But perhaps your father did wrong."

"Where is the wrong? From my balcony I saw a hunted creature stumble through our door and you have hidden him from an officer. Will you give him up, if they come for him?"

Louie Toy rubbed his palms in perplexity.

"He is blood-guilty, Sen Chee. He must pay the penalty."

"Why?"

"It is the rule of our great society that the blood of an enemy is the toll of blood-guilt. These white brothers of ours have laws that must be obeyed. He has taken a life, he must pay the toll."

"Then why did you protect him, my father?"

His eyelids drooped. He folded his arms.

"I scarcely know, doll-child; my heart made a fool of my brain."

"Let us see him. He may have a different story to tell."

Louie Toy hesitated, scowled at his daughter, then walked to the head of the stairway and spoke a guttural command in the Chinese tongue.

A moment later Fong Toon appeared, followed by another Oriental, who drew back in alarm as the daylight struck his eyes, and glanced timorously about the store. Louie Toy's mouth opened in amazement, but his daughter's lips parted from a different cause and a peal of laughter caused his frown to deepen.

"Good old Fong Toon," she cried. "Good old Fong. See, my father, he has dressed the boy in the clothing of Wing Gee. He is only a boy. Why he is not a year older than I, and he looks like one of your clerks. Why, even Fong has parted with his queue, and it would take sharp eyes to pick this man out from one of our own people."

"Such wisdom is for your elders," sneered Louie, disgruntled. "Dress him in his own clothes, Fong Toon, and turn him into the street. I have spoken." He turned away and spat in disdain, heedless of the Mexican's imploring eyes.

The boy, although he could not understand a word of the Oriental tongue, felt intuitively the undercurrent that had turned against him, and his cheeks paled.

Sen Chee, watching him closely, pattered across the floor and laid her hand on her father's arm.

"Wait," she murmured in English, then turned to the boy. "What has happened, did you kill; tell me, did you kill?"

Tears sprang to his eyes and he stretched out his hands. In the soft light his face looked drawn and haggard, and even Louie grunted in grudging pity. Again the Chinese maiden spoke. "Trust us, we will not harm you. Did you fight and kill?"

"No, no, no! I did not mean to keel. She was—she was my, what you call, my girl, and I am jealous, oh so jealous. I did not mean to keel!"

He pressed his hand to his eyes as if to shut out an evil vision, and the girl stepped forward and stroked his head gently.

"Tell us your story. Do not fear. My father is your friend,—I am your friend."

A subtle thrill of magnetism seemed to touch his inner consciousness and, with a movement of decision, he lifted his head and looked into her eyes.

"Why, why—how shall I say, *Señorita?*—no, *Mees,—Mees!*—I am knife thrower at the Hippodrome theater on Pacific street. My *muchacha*, my girl, my Carlotta, she stand before the board and I pin the knives around her, every place, just so. *Si!* I don't hurt her, I don't touch her, but I pin her hair to the planks, I fasten the bow on her shoulder to the boards, I make her skirt to draw tight about her limbs, the knives flash everywhere; *Dios meo*, I miss her one leetle half inch, one-quarter, but I not hurt her. We work at that Hippodrome one week, then one big Americano, what you call tough, he buys for her the *aguardiente*. I ask that she not go, but she drink with him, and she drink again and she drink again; and when we perform her eye is not steady and I am afraid—ah, so much afraid—that I miss, and I throw wild, and I am clumsy, and the peoples laugh at me and I hate them,—ah I hate them, I hate them, I hate them!"

He paused for breath and Louie stirred impatiently, but Sen Chee's warning clasp tightened on his arm.

"Then she take more drink with that *perro,* that beast of an Americano. She no wait for me to-day, but walk out of the theater with heem, with heem,—and I follow them. They stop by the *Carnaceria* at the bottom of Clay street and I wait no longer. I pull the knife from my belt and throw it at that sneering *puerco;* but she see it flash and swing her arm quick, *si,* and the point drive deep in her bosom. A—a—ah!—I know only to run when she scream; and they try to kill me and then you let me stay, and I am safe. I will go, I will go, if you say; they no catch me now. I not care anyway, if my Carlotta is dead!"

He sank down on the floor, a miserable heap of dejection that could not but appeal to even the stolid Celestial's bosom.

Louie Toy's impassiveness slipped from him like a suddenly discarded garment and the Oriental languor was for once replaced by American action.

"Fong Toon," he commanded sharply, "keep this boy below the stairs. Let him unpack the crates that the China steamers bring, and give him to eat of our fare as long as he shall choose to stay."

He turned to his daughter.

"Is my Lily Flower pleased? Perhaps the man is not blood-guilty. I will send a messenger to Ming Tai. Ming is in touch with the police devils and their affairs. He will tell us what we would know. My daughter, my Sen Chee, is she pleased?"

He found his answer deep in the pupil-pools of her eyes. It was a time for silence and, with that one look of understanding, she pattered away and for an hour or more her attention was divided between the folding and replacing of a pile of embroidered mandarin coats in their show-case and the dusting of sundry grotesque images of bronze and ivory that graced her father's shelves.

Her task completed, she seated herself on an ebony stool and leaned upon the glass show-case, staring pensively at a group of strolling sight-seers beyond the doors. Suddenly her shoulders stiffened, her lips parted, and her cheeks colored prettily. A tall Chinese, dressed in ordinary garb, but with hawk-like nose and sharply chiseled features, stood at the window. He made no pretense of examining the goods displayed, but looked at her boldly, and as her lashes fluttered downward in confusion, the lines of his face relaxed in a quizzical smile. Then, as if aware of some hidden menace, he turned away and shuffled aimlessly down Dupont street.

Sen Chee sat for a moment, breathing tensely. Romance was close at hand. She knew that the man belonged to an inimical tong, but for the last three weeks he had stared in at her father's window every afternoon, and once, as she stood at the door, he had whispered her name. A subtle influence gripped her, her heart beat faster, and she murmured a name, harsh to American ears but one that spelled sweet incense to her Oriental soul, "Luk Chan!"

Luk Chan, a member of the Bo Sing Tong, her father's enemies.

Montague and Capulet, reincarnated. The prototypes of Shakespeare's drama of a rose-scented past, modernized and set in a twentieth century frame, with a scenario constructed of the wiles, the intrigues, the plots, and the counterplots of San Francisco's Chinatown.

A "hop-head" slunk around the corner of Clay street and, with furtive eyes on the alert for a "cop," slipped into a den in Waverly Place. His lips were drooling, his cheeks ashen, his straggly beard unkempt. He must have a "shot" of dope, or collapse on the sidewalk.

A half-drunken bum, in tattered overalls, with hat drawn low over his eyes, grunted as the creature passed him, then, as a harsh jangle of discordant sound broke on his ear, lurched to a hydrant at the curb and swayed there in sodden interest. A Chinese dignitary had died, and his funeral cortége was passing along Dupont street. The driver of a closed carriage scattered devil papers with one hand and drove with the other; four musicians made the afternoon hideous with shrieking flageolets and crashing cymbals. A score of male figures, clad in faded purple with white cowls drawn over shaven polls, followed afoot and a dozen sad-faced women shuffled after them. Several hacks, filled with silken-clad mandarins, brought up the rear.

Officer Mulcahey strutted around the corner. His jaw protruded as he saw the reeling bum, but as he peered more closely his countenance changed, he drew his eyelid down in a significant wink, and passed on.

A Chinaman, who had been studying the flaming black-scrawled bulletin upon a dead-wall near the corner, turned nonchalantly and ambled out upon the cobbled street. The vagrant eyed him sleepily. As the procession passed he bent forward, muttered a low word to one of the cowled figures, a wrist shot out from his greasy sleeve and a tiny green slip changed hands. It was done in the twinkling of an eye, but the bum swore tensely.

The Chinese slipped away into the crowd and shuffled off in the direction of Waverly Place. The drunken man lurched after him and clutched at a telegraph pole to steady himself as another green slip changed hands at the doorway of Fong Wing's shoe store. Down to Jackson street and to a clam-depot in a reeking basement, where, by a timely lurch past the cellar stairs the hulking loafer caught again a glint of green. The action was repeated a half-dozen times. A butcher store, an itinerant cobbler, a fruit-stall, a druggist's, a jewelry shop, and Ming Tai's fish market were all visited, and palm met palm to interchange a slip of green.

Once the Chinese twisted his head, and a quick glance over his shoulder showed the uncouth figure that swayed in drunken aimlessness along the walk. His eyes glinted, but after a hesitant step he shuffled on his way, and presently ascended a flight of stairs that led him to a garret in Spofford Alley.

As he disappeared from view the man that had taken so much interest in his proceedings seemed inclined to rest. He sank down in a doorway and, with head bent to his knees and hands trailing drunkenly on the boards, mumbled broken snatches of a ditty of the dives and cursed the slippered Mongolians as they passed him by.

Officer Mulcahey, patrolling his beat, saw the sodden creature, and swore at him in turn. He drew his night-stick and, leaning over, prodded the man in the ribs, calling upon him loudly to move on; but on the heels of his words he flashed a quick query, "What's doin', Bray?"

His victim protested raucously, but between his broken sentences Mulcahey got his answer: "The Bo Sings are up to deviltry. Fow Yuen has delivered a message to at least a dozen hatchet-men. I've got 'em all marked. There's going to be a tong war as sure as hell."

Mulcahey jerked the "vag" to his feet and guided his reeling footsteps to the corner. He led him for half a block down Jackson street, man-handling him as they went, while scurrying Celestials stopped to laugh at the prisoner's maudlin antics before they darted into the doorways of their homes.

Then he released his arm and with a vigorous kick propelled him down the hill.

"'Twas nately done," he mumbled, as he picked a sweet mandarin orange from its tray on a sidewalk fruit-stand and laughed at the grimacing vender who dared not protest.

The drunken bum, otherwise Detective Sergeant Bray, of the Harbor police station, covered many more lengths of sidewalk than were necessary before he turned into a doorway on Washington street, just above Kearney, and mounted the stairs with a far more elastic step than he had been practicing for the last half-hour. He drew a key from his pocket and bent over in the darkened hallway to fit it to its latch. Just as it turned, with a click, something soft fluttered over his face and was drawn tight about his mouth and nostrils. He attempted to cry out, but a pungent odor sickened him and stilled his senses. Some sharp object was thrust against the small of his back, his elbows and knees were gripped in a viselike clutch, and a grunt of satisfaction fell on his ear as his consciousness left him.

A moment afterward four Chinese carried his trussed-up form through a dingy corridor that opened into a blind alley just off Jackson street.

One of their number peered into the outer world for an instant, then their burden was borne through ten feet of daylight, whence they dived into a basement door, and after several windings and descendings and ascendings of short flights of stairs, the unconscious man was deposited in the corner of a room, reeking of opium fumes, where a wizened Chinaman, with scanty gray hair streaking his dirt-grimed face, nodded sagely and whispered a word of commendation.

Evidently the Bo Sing Tong meant business.

CHAPTER II

THE TESTING OF LUK CHAN

Facing a dead-wall at the rear of St. Mary's Cathedral which travesties the barbaric rites of San Francisco's Chinatown by standing, a massive Christian sentinel, at the very threshold of heathenism, practised openly and with more Oriental deviltry in its circumscribed western limits than may be known within the Great Wall of the Flowery Kingdom, a little railed balcony hung for two window-lengths above a cemented court.

The dead-wall was the back of a joss-house, and the balcony marked the second story of the domicile of Sen Chee.

Her father's clerks were putting up shutters; curious sightseers were drifting away to the more sensuous pleasures of the tenderloin dance-halls and the allurement of the underworld.

The spire of St. Mary's pointed its black finger at a moonlit, star-flecked sky, and a silver glow softened the shadows of the court.

Sen Chee's window swung open silently and Louie Toy's "Lily Flower" fluttered out upon the balcony. Fluttered indeed, for the sleeves of her kimono rustled their silken folds and as she tossed her arms above her head they slipped downward, displaying delicately moulded arms, and the scintillant gleam of a jewel flashed in the jade circlet about her wrist. She clasped her hands back of her head and stood for a moment looking at the wall, as if she could see some beckoning image in its dun-colored depths. She was alone with her thoughts.

The moon shone in her eyes, but they beheld only Fancy's image and she dwelt in the Vale of the Thousand Years, the Chinese maiden's realm of love.

At last her lips parted in a sigh, her arms dropped to her side, and the heavy fragrance of the Narcissi, ranged along the railing in their quaint majolica pots, appealed to her senses. She leaned over, brushed her face against the golden heart of a lily, then crushed its petals against her lips and broke its stem. Holding the flower, she moved to the end of the balcony and seated herself in a wicker chair, just outside the low-silled window. Her form was dimly outlined against the fretwork of the rail, but her robe of blue blended with the cloud-flecked moonlight and was merged into invisibility against the dark background of the open window. Again the sigh and a little timorous whisper, "Luk Chan," and the lily was held close against her bosom. A half-hour passed and, lulled by the languorous spell of perfumed air and star-dust falling aslant the moonbeams, her body relaxed. She sank back in her chair; tired lashes drooped upon her cheeks. Her bosom rose and fell to the cadence of her breathing, and she was slipping away to the world of dreams and love, when she was startled by a sharp thud inside the railing and she rose with a cry.

A long bamboo pole rested with its thickest end upon her balcony and slanted to the top of the opposite wall, a dozen feet above, She turned, trembling, to her window, but her step was arrested by a warning "S-sh!" and the low calling of her name. The head and shoulders of a man were outlined upon the roof above, and, though her senses commanded flight, her heart stayed the impulse.

As she faltered there was a swish of rustling garments, a form slid down the pole, and, lips parting in a sweet fear, she looked into the desiring eyes of Luk Chan.

The eighteen years of her life were as nothing to the eternity of his gaze. He held her fascinated. She knew that her heart had passed into the keeping of her father's enemy; and though the lips of Chinese lovers do not meet, their souls were wedded in a kiss of mutual understanding. The silence made the moment more impressive.

A somber setting, one that might not appeal to the American Romeo. But Louie Toy's daughter knew that her future was sealed.

At last the silence was broken.

"Sen Chee, I have waited for seven nights upon the roof." His tone denoted possession; the mastery of it gripped her.

She moved to the rail. "I, too, have sat upon my balcony for twice seven nights and more."

His eyes glinted. "But I could not come to you. One night your father smoked in the court. Another, he talked of business deals with old Ming Tai.

Ming Tai! Ming Tai is a *gow*.[2] Another, Fong Toon burned incense beneath your balcony till I cursed the fragrant joss-sticks, and you were gone before he ceased his mumblings. Something, always something, kept me from you. Last night I leaned over the wall to call your name, but the foreign *Tsai* that was saved from the Police Devils stood in the window at your back for an hour, though you knew it not, and he dodged from sight when you crossed the sill."

"But you came, you came at last! I knew you would come some day, Luk Chan."

He bent over her fiercely.

"It was my love calling to you, Sen Chee. I stood at the window of your father's store day after day, and though you fought against your heart, my eyes mastered you. Sweet Lily Flower, my blue lily of Penang, the rarest blossom of Cathay, tell me that I will wear you in my bosom through the Vale of the Thousand Years, that you will follow me wherever I may go, that you will leave your home, your father, and your friends, and dwell in happiness where I will not be the despised Luk Chan, member of a warring tong, a hatchet-man, an outcast, but Tsue Hei, a lineal descendant of the great Chong Wing, a prince of the royal dynasty. You will be my princess and our children will be of the blood-royal."

A silence fell upon them, his arms were folded across his bosom, he devoured her with his eyes.

A light click behind the girl caused her to start in alarm, and her lover thrust his hand quickly in his blouse.

She stepped to her window and stared intently beyond the casing.

At last she moved to his side and laid her hand upon his shoulder. He thrilled with the touch, his arm slipped around her waist, and he drew her to him cruelly.

"'Twas but the latch slipped," she murmured, and relaxed happily in his embrace.

"Do you love me, doll-child!" he whispered. He felt her soft breath upon his cheek.

"My Luk Chan! Does the water-lily love the pebbles to which it clings? You are my master. Whether you are Tsue Hei, a mandarin of royal blood or a

---

[2] Dog.

tong-man, my father's enemy, it matters not to me. You will always be Luk Chan, the lover of my dreams. Where you go, I will go; where you die, I will die. I have gone to the American schools, I have learned the language of the white people, but now I remember but one word of all their teaching—"

"And that word is—"

"Love!"

A hoarse cry escaped him; then, of a sudden, he released her and sprang back to the rail.

A door closed in the chamber and soft footfalls were heard beyond the sill.

Quick as a flash she darted to the rail, lifted the bamboo pole, and dropped it into the court below.

He flashed a look of doubt at her, but she seated herself in the chair by her window.

"Kneel beside me," she commanded, and, comprehending, he dropped to the floor and crept behind her, huddling close against the wall as she spread out the flowing skirt of her kimono and draped her loose sleeve over the rail.

A filmy cloud crept across the face of the moon as Louie Toy stepped out upon the balcony, thinking dreamily of the comfortable evening he was about to pass there in the fragrant air.

He peered about him for a moment, then spoke chidingly.

"My daughter sits up late. The air is damp. It is life for the lilies, but not for my Lily Flower."

She laughed. "My father often sits till mid-night in the court below. He smokes and chats with Ming Tai long after I have gone indoors."

Louie scowled. "You have man-wisdom, Sen Chee. But I will smoke here for a half-hour to-night."

He waved his bamboo pipe.

"Go within, and let me have your chair."

A slight movement at her side caused her to answer hurriedly:

"No, no, my father. The smoke will come in through my window. The night is too warm to keep it closed. I am tired and the air soothes me." She pouted. "I have folded and unfolded rolls of pongees all day long; I have shown vases of Satsuma and Cloisonne to your customers until I am sick of it all. Let me be in peace to-night, just to-night, my father, or instead of your 'Lily Flower' I fear you will call me your 'Tiger Lily,' for you will find that I have a will of my own."

He grumbled, but she waved her arm at him in mockery.

"My balcony is sacred,"—petulantly,—"I will not have it profaned by smoke, save of fragrant incense. Why, my lilies will sicken and may die. Even now the horrid fumes are curling from your pipe-bowl. Go, before I snatch it from you and throw it over the rail." She made a gesture as if to arise and he clutched his pipe, grimacing amusedly.

"You wear a strange mood to-night, my daughter." He chuckled, then turned abruptly and vanished through the window.

They listened, palpitant, to his shuffling footfalls, and when the doors closed Luk Chan rose stiffly and swayed against the railing, while needle-points of pain darted through his cramped limbs.

His avenue of escape was closed; the pole was gone. His life might pay the penalty of the invasion of Louie Toy's home.

He looked questioningly at Sen Chee, but found no comfort in her smile.

She leaned toward him, pressed some soft object into his hand, and as he stood there stupidly, she slipped away from him, flitted through the casement, and he held the balcony alone.

He opened his fingers and stared at a crushed Narcissus in his palm. Its pungent odor assailed him. Its four fragrant petals spelled "Hope," and, with the flicker of a smile, he stowed it in his bosom. The movement told him that his heart was thumping with a kindling fear.

It meant tragedy to stay until the daylight came, yet he was powerless to go, caught like a rat, a plague rat, who would not be given a flicker of a chance for life.

Something touched his side and he sprang from it, with a shuddering cry of fear.

A blunt object waved before his eyes. He glared at it. It was the end of his bamboo pole. He peered over the rail and in the dim light saw Juan Lucero, the fugitive Mexican, garbed as a Chinese, stretching on tiptoe as he reached aloft.

He raised the pole and the boy slunk away.

He set it on end, braced it firmly between the two walls, and climbed its slanting length to the roof beyond. Then he drew it up after him, and the moon shone on the deserted balcony and its nodding lilies.

A narrow staircase, with two dark and twisted turns, led to the second story of a building in Waverly place.

The night following Luk Chan's escape over the joss-house roof a Chinaman slipped through the entrance, shuffled up the stairs, and tapped on an iron door that seemed strangely out of place in the ramshackle structure. A wicket grated, two slant eyes surveyed him through the slit, and he mumbled a significant phrase in Chinese. Oiled bolts slid back, the door creaked open, and he dived inside. The clang of the closing portals greeted a second Chinaman mounting the stairs.

A similar proceeding ensued, and for a half-hour thereafter flitting Celestials appeared at regular intervals in the hall, but none were turned away, and none arrived in company with others of their kind.

The scene beyond the doorway was strangely at variance with its squalid approach.

A small anteroom opened into a great hall, fully ninety feet in length. It was hung with embroidered draperies. Scaly dragons fought with hideous giants, and the figures of the combatants were worked out in threads of gold; somnolent storks stood on one leg beneath gorgeous clusters of wistaria etched on backgrounds of black satin.

Flaming red banners, with festoons of silken flowers, depended from the ceiling. Ranged along three walls were low ebony stools set with mother-of-pearl. The hardwood floor was bare, but its dun surface shone with a ruddy gloss. Grim figures in Chinese armor, wielding battle-axes of a period long gone by, stood at intervals between the stools and added a somber touch to the setting.

There were at least two hundred of the seats, but each one was occupied by a taciturn Chinese. Some were richly caparisoned, but the majority wore the nondescript garments of the middle-class Chinaman, the small shop-keeper, the fruit and fish peddler, typical representatives of the motley crowd of Mongols that flit incessantly up and down Dupont street during the busy hours of each working day.

At the end of the hall, on a raised platform, were three heavily ornamented chairs, with high backs, decorated with gold and mother-of-pearl.

In the largest one was seated a hideous image, at least eight feet high, fashioned of wood, gaudily painted and dressed in bright silken robes. In the center of its forehead was set a huge staring eye, and the scarlet lips, drawn back in a malign grin, displayed two short tusks projecting over the chin.

On a stand in front of its knees stood a brazen censer, from which sticks of incense emitted fragrant smoke and dropped their ashes into its bowl. Solemnity pervaded the place.

The muttering voices were stilled as a hanging beyond the chairs was drawn aside and a tall Chinese, with a straggling beard, and clothed in a heavily brocaded purple robe, strode into the room.

It was Tom Chong, high chief of the Bo Sing Society, and the members of the tong rose to their feet and stood in reverent silence as he passed before the image and kowtowed in deference before he seated himself at the god's right hand.

He was followed by a wizened creature in ill fitting garb of faded gray silk, who bobbed to the idol, then slipped into the chair at its left, seemingly making an effort to efface himself in its depths.

Tom Chong lifted an ebony block and gave a single tap upon the stand. His auditors seated themselves as one man, and he rose majestically.

"Men of the Bo Sing Tong," he began, "we have been at peace for two blossomings of the Sacred Lily. The great Joss has smiled upon us, but now his brow is wrinkled in a frown. Prosperity has blessed us, our rule has been all powerful, but there has come a rift in the truce. You have answered the call of the Green Dragon, and the Dragon spells blood. The penalty of disobedience to our command is death and we are disciples of Hei De. We are powerless when he exerts his will."

He paused and turned to the figure in the farther chair.

"Ming Tai, priest of the Green Dragon, what business calls our tong-men here to-night?"

Ming Tai slipped from the edge of his seat and puckered his face in a sinister smile,—Ming Tai, fish dealer in the day; moving spirit of a powerful tong at its midnight meetings; professed friend of Louie Toy, a member even of the same tong, though none but Tom Chong knew that he had dared to take the oath of an inimical society that he might spy out its secret plans; treacherous as a snake; evil as a toad; with as many coats as a chameleon.

"Chosen of the gods, your rule has been defied," he muttered, in a cracked voice, but the stillness was so intense that he could be heard to the extreme end of the hall. "Just tribute has been demanded, and it has been refused."

"Who dares to set his will against the mandates of Bo Sing?

"Louie Toy," crisped the voice of Ming Tai; and one Chinese in the gathering started perceptibly, then settled back in affected nonchalance against the wall.

The little Celestial's eye caught the movement and his lips set grimly.

The man who started was Luk Chan.

"Our agent demanded three thousand taels as the price of everlasting protection. Three thousand taels is a small sum to one so wealthy as Louie Toy; but he has ever been a miser save in the affairs of his girl-child, Sen Chee." Again he flashed a glance at Luk Chan. "According to the rule of our society the sum was thrice demanded and each time was refused. At the last he spat upon our gods and consigned them to the chambers of eternal torture. He laughed at our threats and declared that the peace would never be broken,— that the Police Devils would protect him and that we were pallid *gows,* who would be compelled to lick his hand."

An angry buzz rose in the hall, but the high chief stilled it with a commanding gesture.

"My brothers," he said, "Ming Tai speaks with a straight tongue. We dwell together in love, but we rule through fear. He who defies us must die or our organization and its purposes will fail. We live in prosperity through the tributes of the rich, but each one of us is sworn to carry death in his hand when he is called."

He looked at the hatchet-men in silence for a full minute and some of them moved uneasily. Indeed, they nearly all did.

"There is but one chance for life when our will is thwarted. The sentence of doom is beyond the power of human hands. Louie Toy's fate rests with our God, Hei De."

He turned to the priest.

"Ming Tai, repeat our invocation, and we will abide by the sign."

His ally shuffled to the idol's feet and crouched before it, resting his head upon its wooden knees and clasping its ankles as he mumbled an interminable chant, while the assemblage gazed fascinated at the spectacle.

Of a sudden a suppressed murmur broke the silence, and the tong-men stood in awe.

The lid of the image's staring eye drooped slowly until it was entirely closed, and, though Ming Tai rambled on for five minutes or more, it masked the glass orb, and the fanatical Chinese sat spellbound.

At last the high priest ceased his mutterings and, as he crept exhausted to his chair, Hei De's eyelid raised with startling rapidity.

Tom Chong lifted his hand.

"You have witnessed the token. Louie Toy must die. Let the lots be drawn."

Ming Tai recovered his poise in the twinkling of an eye and, leaving the platform, lifted a brazen urn from its stand and shuffled down the line of Celestials.

Each man, as he halted before him, thrust a hand beneath his blouse and drew forth a tiny green slip, depositing it in the urn.

A slip was collected from all in the room save two, Tom Chong and a young Chinaman, the last member to join the tong.

The new member followed Ming Tai to the altar and, after a cover had been placed on the urn and it had been shaken vigorously, a silken scarf was bound across his eyes.

When the lid was lifted Ming Tai clutched his arm and held it over the fateful receptacle.

He stood hesitant for a moment, then thrust his hand quickly into the depths and drew forth a single green slip.

The high chief, Tom Chong, took it from his fingers.

In tense silence his dupes watched his lips.

"Luk Chan!" he said at length, and cast the slip back into the urn.

Quietly the lover of Sen Chee rose and took his station before the joss, where the blood-oath was administered,—the oath that compelled him to slay her father within the fortnight, or to meet death himself at the hands of his tong.

Though something deep within his bosom cried out against the hideousness of it all, though it hurt him so cruelly that he could scarcely breathe, he repeated the oath with a stoic's tongue; and Ming Tai, staring cynically in ill concealed dislike, saw nothing to find fault with.

CHAPTER III

THE INCENSE VENDER

Ming Tai laid down the knife with which he had been cleaning sand-dabs, wiped his hands on a gunny-sack, and pulled on a blouse over his odorous jersey.

He muttered something in Chinese to his assistant, tucked a brown paper parcel under his arm and left his fish-stall, going down Clay street to the plaza. He took a diagonal cut across the park, turned up Jackson street, and dived into a little alley, scarcely a dozen feet wide, between tall buildings.

The cul-de-sac was deserted, and he scuttled down some stairs into a basement entrance. He knocked loudly at two or three different doors in a twisting hallway, waiting for an instant at each and smiling as his summons brought no response. At last he stopped at a door near the end and tapped upon the panel. He rapped a second time, calling in Chinese, then he rattled the knob and walked in. Throwing his bundle on a table in a corner, he turned to go, when his steps were arrested by a sort of sobbing sound, like the moan of some animal in distress.

A guttural exclamation evidenced his surprise and he faced about, peering into the gloom.

Ming Tai was an actor; his visit had been carefully planned. His summons at the various doors, the package of fish, and its delivery were simply ruses used to produce the effect of an innocent approach.

He took a match from his blouse and lighted a gas-jet, whose flare showed him an inert form lying face downward against the wall. He stooped, rolled the figure over on its back, and looked into the purpled face of the detective.

"Sargen' Blay!" he exclaimed, then drew a knife from his girdle and cut the rope that bound the officer's arms and ankles and tore a bandage from his lips and eyes.

The prisoner groaned, but was beyond the power of motion.

Ming Tai dropped to his knees and began to rub the cord-marked wrists vigorously.

"Wha's malla, Sargen'?" he said. "You try catchem tief; tief he plenty catchem you?"

"Thief be damned!" growled Bray. "This is tong business. What are you doing here?" suspiciously.

Ming Tai's answer was childlike.

"Oh, this my pidgin. Me catchem orders for flatfish, for sole, for flounder; you savey. Me bling 'em here to Hip Lung. You know Hip Lung?"

"No!"

The Chinaman cackled. "Hip Lung he smoke um hop. Him no go out. Me bling em fish twice one week."

"Well, he's gone out to-day."

"Yes. Mebbe him collect lent. Him landlord. This him tenement."

Bray rose to a sitting posture dizzily.

"Well, I'm damned glad you happened along. What do you know about this business? What tong does Hip Lung belong to?"

The Chinaman bent double, cackling in mirth. Not often was he so amused.

"Hip Lung him not hatchet-man. Him poor. Spend all him money for *ah-peen-yeen*. He smokem dope. P'leeceman he no catch. Hip Lung too fly."

The detective sergeant glared his disgust. He knew that there was not a possible chance to fasten the guilt of his imprisonment on one of these wretched creatures. They would swear to anything in court; their plans had been craftily laid, and he had not set eyes on one of his captors. Ming Tai's visit was an innocent one. He was helpless. Evidently their schemes had been put through and he was no longer a menace. Hence his release.

He determined to temporize. He did not known Ming Tai to be a highbinder; he had always played up to the police and had, at times, placed him on the scent of an important capture.

He was really in the Mongol's debt, more so through his present action. But some deviltry was afoot among the tongs; he would learn what he could.

"Good old Ming," he said, "you're a pretty white Chink. I won't forget this. Mebbe I can get you out of a scrape sometime."

Ming grinned blandly.

"What's going on in Waverly Place? Come, through with it now! You know something's up."

The old fish dealer raised his palms in protest.

"Him not my pidgin, Sargen' Blay. Me no catchem what you mean."

The detective bluffed. "Oh, yes you do. I spotted a highbinder yesterday peddling green slips. That's a blood call, Ming."

His auditor chattered in alarm.

"No, no, you makee mistlake! Who you see catchem?"

Bray scratched his head. "Well, I didn't recognize any of the Chinks. But there was a lot of tickets handed out. Wait! By God, there was one highbinder that I spotted! Luk Chan got a green ticket. You know Luk Chan?"

The detective was on his feet by this time, stamping his swollen limbs and cursing his vanished captors.

Ming lied blithely. "Oh, yes, me know Luk Chan. Luk Chan belong Hop Sing Tong." Purposely he accredited membership in Louie Toy's society to the man he hated, and drew suspicion from his brothers of the Bo Sings.

Bray pounded the table. "I knew something was doing. I'll post the chief and we'll have a squad of policemen detailed to watch the Hop Sings."

Ming Tai's face wrinkled. He wanted to laugh aloud, but he masked his feelings. "Sargen' Blay heap good flen'. He protect poor old Ming from highbinders. Ming he not forget. He watchem China boy. He tell him all about Luk Chan!"

"All right; you won't lose by it. Let's get out of here. The smell of the hop's got my goat."

Ming led the way and they stumbled along the narrow hall. When they came to the stairway he stepped aside.

"You go first, Sargen'. Me no likee they see us same pidgin."

Bray growled an assent, mounted the stairs and, leaving the alley, turned down Jackson street toward Kearney.

An ancient incense-vender, with a tray strapped about his neck, brushed by him, but he gave no heed.

Ming Tai slipped from the shadow of the buildings and shuffled up the hill. The vender halted by a lamp-post and muttered an imprecation in Chinese as the fish peddler rounded the corner and turned into Dupont.

The vender of incense would have been a tall man of his race had he not been so stooped with age. His body, bent almost double over his tray, was clad in rags; bare toes peeped through his sandals; and his scant trousers flapped about naked ankles. His blouse was gathered over a dirt grimed bosom, his neck was streaked and scrawny; thin wisps of gray hair straggled from under the rim of a slouch hat, much too large for him, that was pulled down low on his head, concealing his queue and shading his eyes; his checks were ashen where they showed through the deeper stains of dirt, and his hands were of a hue beyond description.

His tray was laden with papered packets, and a half-dozen tiny storks, of green metal, standing long-legged on lily-pads, were arranged along the front. In the bill of each was stuck a stick of incense, from which fragrant smoke arose as the ashes crumbled and glowed.

It was after sunset when Ming Tai disappeared around the corner and the shadows were lengthening. The ancient vender leaned against his post for a time, his eyes closed, his gaunt figure swaying. Apparently some lotus dream of a happier past took his thoughts from present misery, for he smiled and mumbled to himself. At last he straightened a trifle and crept painfully up the hill, hurrying Chinamen scarce condescending to keep out of his way and paying no heed to the querulous voice in which he cried his wares.

He turned into Dupont and headed southward, toward old St. Mary's. After fifteen minutes of painful progress, during which he entered one or two stores, he stopped before the Canton Bazaar. This had been his destination all along.

He blinked at the windows for a time, then pressed the latch and shuffled inside.

Louie Toy was displaying mandarin coats to some American tourists when the grating voice fell on his ear, and looking up, he spied the peddler. His persuasive smile changed to a frown and he spoke sharply to Fong Toon, who hurried forward from the rear of the store and angrily ordered the old man out. His step was so slow that Fong Toon laid a hand on his shoulder to accelerate his progress, when the motion was arrested by a low spoken word *"ah-peen-yeen."*

The clerk hesitated, then jabbered something in Chinese, and got a quavering answer.

He muttered a quick sentence to Louie Toy, and the merchant dropped the garment he was holding so quickly that his prospective customers stared in astonishment. His answer came back quick as a flash; then he recovered his poise as Fong Toon turned away.

The incense-vender crept along the show-cases, peering at the goods and shaking his head as he droned some queer jargon.

Louie Toy's daughter, seated at the end of the store behind a high counter, watched him with disgust as he sidled in her direction.

However, her Oriental stoicism caused her to sit still as he paused in front of her and the incense wafted its soothing scent to her nostrils.

He mumbled brokenly and nodded over the counter, then, suddenly, he raised his head, looked straight at her and whispered two words, "Sen Chee."

She could hardly suppress a cry, for the eyes that she looked into were not the eyes of age, but wide open, full-pupiled orbs, burning with the fire of youth.

"Luk Chan!" The phrase trembled on her lips, but a sibilant "S-sh!" stilled it, and she shivered at his boldness. An intangible fear crept upon her. Intuition warned her that this visit meant danger. Why, she could not tell. There were easier ways to communicate with her than by the assumption of this elaborate disguise. And she felt that his mission was a dangerous one.

He tottered away and she watched him, fascinated, until Louie Toy's customers were gone.

The merchant could hardly conceal his impatience, and as soon as he had bowed them through the door he closed it with a bang and hurried to the vender's side, questioning him in his mother tongue.

The old man looked about him shrewdly, then suddenly lifted a shallow tray that covered the false bottom of the larger one, and Louie's eyes widened. A broad smile spread over his countenance.

"Ah-peen-yeen," he muttered. Before the vender dropped the tray into place he had seen at least a score of five-tael boxes of opium nestling cozily in their hiding-place. Twenty five-tael boxes of the precious drug. These little oblong boxes were the vision that filled his brain during his waking hours and most of his sleeping ones.

Little boxes, about four inches long by three inches wide and an inch and a quarter thick, pasted over with a dull red paper covered with Oriental characters. Each tin contained six and two thirds ounces of prepared opium, the importation of which has been prohibited for over a year, save for medicinal purposes, and the prohibition is absolute under any circumstance as far as the Chinese merchants are concerned. The value of the drug in the old man's tray was, under present conditions, close to two hundred dollars, and Louie Toy knew that he must be the agent of some lawbreaker that had a large cache safely stowed.

Louie Toy would purchase all that they might bring him. He had a ready market for it at an enormous profit, so he clutched the decrepit creature's arm almost fondly and guided him down the stairs that they might discuss details of the deal in regions below the Police Devils' vision.

Fong Toon remained on guard in the store and gave evasive answers to Sen Chee's queries.

The girl feared for her father and for her lover. Some slip of the tongue might betray Luk Chan and she knew what that would mean. He would never leave the store alive.

There was open enmity between the hatchet-man and Louie Toy.

Surely the visit was portentous of evil.

After an interminable time the oddly variant pair appeared above the stairs, and Louie's eyes held a gleam of satisfaction.

He spoke tersely to Fong Toon, telling him to close the store early and that he would be away for an hour at least. A sense of danger warned Sen Chee to protest, but the habit of ages and knowledge of her father's moods kept her quiet.

The incense-vender seemed to grow taller as they passed out onto the sidewalk and his feebleness fell away from him. Louie Toy noticed no change; his mind was occupied with thoughts of a pungent narcotic at the other end of their journey.

They passed down Dupont street to Clay, and waited in the shelter of an awning for the south-bound car.

Luk Chan's hands trembled, his fingers worked convulsively in his sleeves' depths, but murder must wait on business. There would be time enough for the fulfilment of his vow after Louie had been shown his wares.

They boarded the car and changed at Kearney, crossing the lower portion of the city and leaving it at the Third and Townsend Street Sheds.

They stumbled along the tracks, dodging in and out amongst "dead" freight-cars for a quarter of a mile, emerging at last on a deserted street opposite Pier 42, where the *Korea's* giant bulk loomed darkly in the starlight.

A light showed, bobbing in the bay, and, as they neared the steamer, forms of customs inspectors might be seen pacing the decks, close to the rail.

"You tell me six hundred five-tael tins were brought ashore from the *Korea*, and the white searchers were baffled? It is hard to believe," whispered Louie Toy. "Why, they know all the hiding-places; they prod with their long rods, they even hunt amongst the coal. Three great ships have come from China within the month, and from no one of these has a single box escaped their eyes. Have the inspectors been bribed?"

The vender grinned in a knowing way.

"No; they were outwitted. Two cabin stewards share our profits. A pig's bladder, holding four tins of *ah-peen-yeen* packed in soft cotton-wool, was placed in each of fifty pillows used in the sleeping berths. The White Devils slept soundly and perhaps dreamed of poppies. When the ship tied up to her dock the stewards sent their pillows ashore to be cleaned, and Pon Him, my master, cleaned them."

Louie chuckled. "Pon Him cleaned them well. But the balance?"

"It was hidden beneath the cabin stairs. Four hundred tins of it. Each stair is covered with a brass plate, fastened with rows of tiny screws. They little know how our friends worked for three long nights with those brazen plates. You shall see how they are delivering the drug."

The bay-shore has been filled in for its entire dockage length, and the approaches to the piers consist of rough planking, under which the tide water laps the sand and rocks that have been dumped into the ooze.

The old vender led his companion a few steps along the boards, then squatted down, felt about with his fingers, and turned a loose plank on edge. Through an opening wide enough to admit a man's body a noisome odor greeted them. He whistled twice and, presently, a light flickered below them, a guttural challenge was satisfactorily answered, and before he could realize it Louie Toy was being lowered below the wharf. The lantern was extinguished, and a hand on either side guided him.

He stumbled along a hundred yards in the darkness and halted, at a low command.

A hood was whisked from another lantern hanging to an upright and he found himself in a sort of hollowed out den, from which a little tunnel led toward the bay.

A Chinaman began to pile loose tins of opium on a blanket, and the incense-vender pointed at two gleaming wires, of scarcely the thickness of a thread, that were fastened to the post. As he looked something whirred along the strand. Waiting hands clutched a tiny basket containing six tins of *ah-peen-yeen*.

"An open port in the *Korea's* bow and two good friends inside," whispered the vender.

Louie Toy nodded. He was thoroughly interested.

"A dozen basket-loads and it will be the end. Is Louie Toy satisfied with what he has seen?"

A vigorous affirmative.

"I will buy the *ah-peen-yeen* as long as you will deliver it to me!"

They waited in silence until the final voyage of the basket; then, at a signal, the wire was loosened at the other end, drawn in and coiled, and the mouth of the tunnel closed with large rocks and loose earth.

A half-hour was spent in dickering. Louie, although he had brought the gold with him, refused at first to pay their price, for fear of treachery. But full payment in advance was demanded, and, fearful that they would sell to another, he at last handed over a clinking bag that had been clutched beneath his blouse for the last hour, and had to put his faith in the word of the incense-vender, whose name even was unknown to him.

"Deliver the tins to Ming Tai's stall at noon," he directed. "Two coolies with fish baskets swinging from their poles, will fool the Police Devils, and Ming Tai will buy their catch."

The Chinaman nodded and he rose. His guide, decrepit once again, grasped his wrist and they groped their way back over the uneven path. Water lapped their sandals, and Louie shivered.

For an unaccountable reason panic seized him, and jerking his arm away from the restraining clutch, he ran toward the patch of light that showed ahead. Just as he reached the opening his foot struck a rock and he fell flat on his face in the sand.

With an oath, Luk Chan, the tong-man, leaped after him. The hour had come.

Louie Toy lay prostrate, the breath driven from his body by his fall.

A small, keen-edged hatchet slipped down from the sleeve of Luk Chan. He gripped its handle and as it swung above his head the gleaming blade flashed in his eyes.

One stroke and his oath was fulfilled.

But even as his arm swooped downward to cleave the skull of his enemy a sweet voice seemed to murmur in his ear, and a moonlit balcony danced within his brain.

"Sen Chee!"

No one spoke. There was no one to speak, to see, to hear. But he could have sworn that he heard the Chinese maiden's name.

His arm dropped to his side. The hatchet slid back into his sleeve, and he helped Louie Toy to rise.

They separated at the freight sheds, and each rode back to Chinatown alone.

CHAPTER IV

FISH ALLEY

Juan Lucero's *muchacha* was not so seriously hurt as the Mexican's pursuers believed. She was hurried to the emergency hospital while Officer Mulcahey and the rabble at his heels were scouring Chinatown for the boy, but beyond a deep knife wound in her shoulder that caused considerable loss of blood and consequent weakness she was in no danger.

After the internes dressed her injury she was removed to the county hospital, where a stay of two weeks was counseled by the head-surgeon. When she had recovered somewhat from the shock and excitement she refused to bring any charge against her assailant, and the police were powerless. The man who had been the cause of it all disappeared, and soon afterward the news traveled by some grape-vine system of the underworld to the frightened creature in Louie Toy's cellar.

He had been working with the Chinamen, garbed as they were, and had kept so still a tongue in his head and labored so docilely that Fong Toon had conceived a strange liking for him, and, in his Oriental way, had sounded his praises to Louie Toy.

When Juan heard of his sweetheart's condition his courage returned, and he sought the manager of the Hippodrome to beg a continuation of his engagement.

The booking-agent of a tenderloin circuit that held several weeks of steady work happened to be in the office, and the possibilities of the act appealed to him.

The morning papers had contained vivid accounts of Lucero's attack on the girl and would furnish a far better "ad" than any press agent could obtain. So an arrangement was made and the boy was billed as a headliner on the dancehall boards.

By the advice of the agent, a dummy figure was used as a target. The programmes announced that "The Great Lucero" would be seen in a "knife-casting exhibition of marvelous skill," and that the same "stiletto that had sapped the lifeblood of Carlotta" would be used by him again.

It appealed to the tenderloin denizens, and the act "went big."

Juan, filled with remorse, thought only of his girl's recovery, and he made daily drafts on his salary, spending it all on dainties that were sent to the hospital.

He was so grateful to the Chinese merchant that he offered to continue his work in the packing room, and Louie, impelled, no doubt, by prescience, let him have his own way. Save for the short intervals when he appeared at the theater, he worked at Fong Toon's crates, and took his meals with the Orientals. A strange proceeding surely, but he was an alien, more of an outcast perhaps than the Mongols with whom he fraternized. There was no mention of pay, and no one concerned thought of it.

One afternoon, while he was hurrying down Jackson street to the theater, he saw Ming Tai talking to Detective Sergeant Bray in front of his fish stall.

Just as he passed them he thought he heard Louie Toy's name spoken, and it impelled him to pause. He bent over, fumbling with his shoelace, and caught a phrase or two in the China man's "pidgin" English. When he straightened, his eyes were glistening, and he mumbled a low sentence in his mother tongue.

What he had heard spelled danger to his benefactor. If he had gone directly to Louie Toy with the tale several lives might have been saved, and much of villainy averted. But the crude workings of the boy's mind were not equal to his problem.

As he walked on down the hill a fantastical plan formed in his brain and he determined to offer himself as a sacrifice on the altar of gratitude. Perhaps he could carry out his idea alone. At least he would try.

Sen Chee was the stumbling-block. He worshiped her for her interference in his behalf, and he would save her father and thwart the schemes of Ming Tai.

During his afternoon performance at the Hippodrome he cast his knives so badly that the stage-manager "gave him a call down" in his dressing-room.

When Lucero returned to the Canton Bazaar he donned his rough, Oriental garb, pulled a slouch hat over his eyes, and slipped out of the basement entrance. Even an expert eye might have failed to detect his identity. He looked exactly like hundreds of other young Chinese who thronged the streets and alleys. Keeping in the shadows, he made his way to Fish Alley and was soon lost to sight amongst the nondescript crowd that moved ceaselessly up and down its sidewalks.

At eleven o'clock Ming Tai's assistants put up his shutters and he went to his till to count his receipts.

The clinking coins slipped through his fingers into a greasy sack and his eyes narrowed into a gleam of pleasure, but they opened suddenly as, picking up a piece of silver, he spied an ivory disk in the bottom of the drawer.

He took it up curiously, rubbed its smooth surface, and turned it over in his palm. The bag fell unheeded to the floor as he stared in amazement at the reverse side. The ivory disk was an insignificant object, but it held much of portent to the old tong-man. Just an ordinary poker chip, white, but etched crudely in red ink on its surface was a tiger-cat (the Chinese name for the California wildcat), with snarling lips, teeth exposed, tail a-curl, back arched, and vicious claws extended. He shot a swift glance at his assistants, but they were chattering innocently. A subtle fear crept over him. He picked up the sack, thrust it beneath his blouse, and stared again at the disk.

Whenever a tiger-cat is killed in the Marin County hills, it is shipped to some San Francisco commission house, and before long becomes the property, at a very fancy price, of some warring highbinder, who eats its heart and throws the carcass away. This may seem absurd to the peaceful inhabitants of an eastern community, but every resident of the western metropolis who is at all versed in the customs of its cosmopolitan population knows it to be a very common rite. The tong-man who eats the heart of a tiger-cat is held in reverence by his fellows, for they know that to do so instils bravery in his bosom and that he will slay without a tremor at the mandate of his tong.

Ming Tai's brow wrinkled. Did the sprawling beast portend evil? No, it was impossible. It was some fetish, some pocket-piece, that had slipped by mistake into his till with the coin of a customer. He snapped it in two between his fingers and threw the broken bits into a garbage can at the rear of the store.

More important business was at hand and he dismissed the incident from his mind.

The exterior of Ming's fish market was innocent enough in the daytime. It was an object of interest to eastern visitors, who saw the great zinc-lined counters, with their burdens of fish,—sun-fish, sand-dabs, barracouta, skates, perch, smelt, sardines, rock-cod, flounders, striped bass,—piled in indiscriminate masses and pawed over throughout the day by the dirty fingers of the bartering Mongols, who bought them at one-third the price they would have paid in the American markets.

Along the wall were heavy wooden crates that held Peking ducks, and below the sidewalk, visible through a wooden grating, hundreds of chickens roosted on bamboo perches, disconsolately awaiting their turn for execution. Yes, it was all very innocent, but the fish and the poultry-stalls furnished the minor part of Ming Tai's income.

He engaged in traffic of another kind after midnight.

Below the store was a large cellar, low-ceiled, with a sawdust sprinkled floor. It contained a score of tables, about which were seated groups of wildly excited Chinese as Ming, after discarding the broken disk of ivory, slipped through a rear door and peered about him, snuffing the smoke-laden atmosphere.

He smiled. Business was good. It was legally conducted too. Under the name of the "Royal Peking Club," gambling of all kinds was licensed. The White Devils could not obtain permits to run gambling-clubs of their own, but the City Fathers winked at and did not interfere with Celestial customs or inclinations, except in the matter of *ah-peen-yeen.*

And many whites visited the Chinese dens, where they could play the lottery, daytime or night-time, and indulge in games of dominoes, pigow, or fan-tan.

Ming Tai, although more prosperous than any inmate of his gambling-cellar, was the most wretched-appearing object in the room. As he shuffled about, with flapping slippers and bent shoulders, mumbling a greeting here and there, his unkempt clothes,—his blouse, marked with a greasy, shining stain between its shoulders from the constant rubbing of his queue,—his twitching hands, pallid cheeks, bleary eyes, marked him rather as a devotee of the opium pipe than one of the most powerful figures in San Francisco's Chinatown. In a smoke-laden corner of the room, ten or a dozen evil-looking Celestials were seated about a table, and Ming took his station by the dealer, watching their play with avaricious eyes. This was one of the most profitable sources of his income.

The dealer stood by a glass jar filled with beans. He would dip his hand into the jar and draw it out full of little white objects that meant so much to the players. They would place their bets on the boards in front of them and he would begin to count: *"Yet! Gee! Som! Sayee!"* ("One! Two! Three! Four!"), dropping a bean on the table at each monosyllable. The excited Chinese shrilled the count with him until the noise was a Babel. The game was to guess whether there would be one, two, three, or none left in his hand after the beans had all been counted out by fours, and although two or three players always won, receiving even money for their bets, the great majority of their coins were raked into the dealer's pile. This was the famous game of fan-tan, played all over the world, wherever a Chinese population may be found. And one redeeming trait of the Chinese is that he never cheats at his gambling.

As Ming was chuckling to himself after a particularly successful hand he heard suddenly the low jangle of a bell and slipped away, going behind a wooden partition and down a gloomy passageway to the rear of the cellar. He tapped on the door-panel, and receiving a peculiar signal in return, shot the bolt.

A woman wearing a dowdy fur coat that was partly hooked, a short skirt of rich material that was stained with wine dregs, and high-heeled shoes and silk stockings, smirked at him brazenly and dropped some clinking coins in his hand as she switched a lace scarf from her head and showed her rouged cheeks and eyes that held the hopelessness of ages. Without a word he faced about, led the way past another turn in the partition, and thrust back a heavy hanging that displayed three bunks, almost identical in appearance with stateroom berths in small coasting steamers.

The upper one was empty, but a partly disrobed Mongol was sprawled in the lower one, breathing heavily, with the leaden whites of his eyeballs showing beneath half-closed lids. A pungent odor hung in the air.

The woman laughed, crawled into the middle bunk, and Ming brought her a tray, which she seized avidly as she rested on her elbow.

He left her, and with trembling fingers she struck a match and lighted a small alcohol lamp. The creature was an opium fiend and the tray contained a hop layout.

She lifted a pipe with a mushroom-shaped bowl, in the center of which was drilled a tiny hole. Then she took a small needle, dipped it into a tin of brown, sticky substance, twisted it into a ball, and held it over the burning wick until it melted and began to run like molten wax. Turning it deftly, she let it trickle into the hole in her pipe and drew a long, languorous inhalation, sighing in satisfaction as the smoke entered her lungs.

A half-dozen times the operation was repeated; then, as she reached for the lamp, her pipe slipped from her grasp, the needle fell unheeded to the floor, and she sank back on her pillow, two spots of rouge glowing upon her sallow cheeks as she entered the land of lotus dreams and unhallowed delights. The spell of poppy juice was upon her and for an hour at least the sordidness of her world was left behind.

If the customs inspectors or the secret service agents could have peeped in behind the hangings, Ming Tai's income and his liberty too might have been suddenly curtailed.

He had already forgotten his customer in the allurements of fan-tan and at the insistence of some of the players had taken the dealer's place. He pushed aside the tin cover of the bean jar, drew up his sleeve and dealt so successfully that the pile of coins before him grew larger and larger, and the voices of the players increased to a discordant medley of broken cries as they hung on the count and watched their bets go glimmering.

A sudden commotion near the door caused him to look up, and a hush fell as the guard ushered in a dignified Chinese. It was Tom Chong, the high chief of the Bo Sing Tong, and his eyes lifted in an almost imperceptible signal to Ming Tai as he passed him and seated himself on a wooden settee in an alcove devoted to the use of Ming's wealthier customers. It was deserted now, and he sat there for a time, puffing his bamboo pipe and waiting for his ally to find an opportunity to join him.

At last, as one or two of the players went "broke" and pushed back their chairs, Ming called to the dealer to take his place, and unconsciously lifted the little tin cover.

The inherent stoicism of his race was all that kept him from crying aloud in terror, for gleaming on the table was a white ivory disk, with a snarling tiger-cat etched across its surface. Instinct came to his rescue and the chip slipped into his palm as the cover clattered to the floor. He picked it up, replaced it, and hurried on trembling limbs to the alcove, where he dropped to a seat alongside of Tom Chong. He tried to conceal the fear that possessed him.

Tom Chong drew away from him as far as the small settee would allow. A slight shudder of repulsion was conquered, and he eyed the old villain curiously.

"What ails you, Ming Tai? Your face is of the hue of incense ashes."

The old Chinaman's visage wrinkled in a smile.

"The burden of years, Tom Chong. And, perhaps, smoke fumes and this foul atmosphere. We dare not have ventilators. The Police Devils might spy on us, or hear sounds not intended for their ears."

Tom Chong grunted. "What have you in your hand?"

Ming repressed a start and opened his fingers.

By good fortune the plain side lay upward and there was nothing significant to the tong-chief's eyes. His henchman would not have aroused his suspicion for all the world. Chong was crafty and a glimpse of the tiger-cat might have put him on his guard and caused him to alter plans whose execution was vital to Ming Tai.

"I found a poker chip amongst the coins. It must have slipped in with some player's bet."

Absently he broke it in two, then snapped each of the halves again between his fingers and threw the bits away. His chief noticed nothing out of the ordinary, but a great fear possessed the fish dealer's soul.

For some reason he was marked, and time alone would reveal the significance of his warning.

Tom Chong's queries came to him through a haze, but at last he pulled himself together and managed to give rational answers.

"Louie Toy still lives," said the high chief at length. "The *ah-peen-yeen* is in your cellars. The price has been paid, but Louie Toy still lives."

Ming Tai shrugged his shoulders.

"It is only the second night since Luk Chan took his blood-oath."

"True. But Luk Chan's orders were plain. And they were not fulfilled."

Ming hastened to agree.

"Why did he not remove our enemy after the money was paid over for his *ah-peen-yeen*? Then you would have fallen heir to the drug, Ming Tai, and none could have disputed your ownership—and mine."

"*Gow!*" muttered the fish dealer. "I know not what went wrong. But it is only a matter of days, Tom Chong. The oath of Luk Chan must be fulfilled before the eleventh Sun, or his life is forfeit." His lip curled. "I would have killed them both, had I been given my way that night at the Mail Dock."

His chief stared.

"Luk Chan is but a tool; we must protect him."

"Bah! I juggled the green slips at our meeting when Luk Chan's name was drawn and I fooled even you. Luk Chan must die."

"Why?"

"He has taken something of Louie Toy's that I desire, that I will have, even if in getting it I disrupt the Bo Sing Tong."

"What do you mean? What has Luk Chan that he has not turned over to you?"

"The heart of Louie's daughter. The heart of Sen Chee."

Tom Chong fell back in his seat astounded, then recovering, he gave vent to a fit of silent laughter that roused his companion's ire.

A figure, crouching in a dark corner of the settee, rose to its feet and glided noiselessly into the larger room, unnoticed by either of the Chinamen.

Ming Tai's anger rose.

"I see no cause for mirth. Sen Chee is young and graceful as a willow. She would make a pretty slave."

"But you have the years of our pagodas, Ming Tai. They should bring you the wisdom of Confucius. Say that this is a jest."

"It is the truth," crustily. "Have I ever claimed any reward for myself during all the years that I have assisted you in the councils of the Bo Sings? I have made you, Tom Chong, a despised outcast, an urchin of the streets, the leader of the most powerful society in this country of the White Devils. You have been their high chief, respected, kowtowed to by men whose feet you are not fit to kiss, men who would spurn you, would spit on you, would cast you out into the gutters, if they knew your ancestry. What have I had of all the years?—I, Ming Tai, the despised peddler of Fish Alley, old and weazened, bent by my toil, hideous even? Yet beneath it all I have a heart and my heart cries out for its desire. I have been too busy through all my life, but now,— yes, even to you I say it,—now my brain has turned to thoughts of love."

A sneer curled Tom Chong's lip, but it died in its inception.

There was a sudden, resounding crash at the street door, the sound of heavy blows and splintering wood, and as the frightened inmates of the gambling-hall dived under tables and scurried for cover like rabbits scuttering to their warrens, the barrier gave way and a squad of police rushed through the opening.

Tom Chong and Ming Tai leaped up and started in opposite directions, but were jerked from their feet and dashed to the floor so abruptly that the breath was driven from their bodies and they gaped stupidly at the men who bent over them, and gasped in agony.

Some one had tied their queues together as they plotted on the bench, and, like Absalom of Biblical days, their hair brought about their downfall.

CHAPTER V

SEN CHEE'S BALCONY

Something was wrong with Sen Chee. Since the night that she recognized Luk Chan beneath the rags of the incense-vender she had drooped like one of the fading lilies on her balcony rail.

Instinct warned her that there was menace in her lover's disguise. His surreptitious journey with her father, the abrupt answer that she received when she questioned Louie Toy, her failure to see the young tong-man since that visit, all combined to worry her.

Her placid life had suddenly changed. Ever since childhood she had been her father's confidante, and now constraint had sprung up between them. With the perverseness of maiden hood, she gave way to the feeling that something evil had befallen Luk Chan.

Perhaps her father had recognized his enemy and had caused one of his agents to make way with him. Else why had he not made his daily visit to their shop-window?

For two long afternoons she had looked for him in vain, and now, sick at heart, she kept her room. She gave petulant answers to her father's queries and begged to be left alone. His eyes beheld but bodily illness; he could not see the sickness of her soul.

Dressed in her flowered kimono, she lay upon her couch, staring at the ceiling and seeing visions of hatchet-men with upraised arms. Dozing fitfully, she would dream of dreadful happenings, would hear a despairing call for help, and would awaken to the blankness of unsympathetic sunlight on a tinted wall.

At last she could stand the strain no longer, and rising with a sigh, stepped across the windowsill and seated herself in the little wicker chair at the corner of her balcony.

The nodding lilies failed to interest her. She looked at the brick wall of the joss-house and thought of a moonlit night when Luk Chan descended suddenly from the heights beyond and whispered to her of love.

She closed her eyes to lock beneath their lids the happiest memory of her life. Once again Luk Chan's voice commanded her to follow him to the ends of the earth and once again she bowed submissive to his will.

"Where you go, I will go, beloved," she murmured. "I will leave my father and his people. Whether you take me to the spice lands of Cathay or to the deathless Vale of the Thousand Years, I shall be content. The Thousand Years are long, but our souls will be purified with waiting, and will dwell thereafter in Eternity. Luk Chan, you are my man and if harm has befallen you at my father's hands I will join you beyond the gates. At Wing Kee's drug store there is an herb that will transport me quickly to the regions where you dwell. Life is death without you, and death will bring me your companionship and love."

Her head sank forward on her bosom and a tear-drop trickled down her cheek.

In her anguish she forgot the flight of time. An hour had passed, and she had sobbed herself into a light doze when she was awakened by the scraping of a chair on the flags below the balcony and the acrid odor of tobacco smoke assailed her nostrils.

A sentence, spoken in a guttural tone, caused her to sit upright suddenly and to grip the arms of her chair.

It was the voice of Ming Tai and it carried a portent of evil.

"What thought you of the incense-vender, Louie Toy? His looks belied his mission."

The merchant chuckled.

"He was unknown to me. But his mission was a fruitful one. We will profit by many taels through the sale of his *ah-peen-yeen*. May his visit be soon repeated."

A load fell from the heart of Sen Chee. That one casual sentence from her father's lips lifted the weight of the universe from her bosom. Luk Chan still lived. He was expected to visit the Canton Bazaar again. If she had been a Christian maid, she would have sung and danced her delight, and thereby caused her lover's downfall. But she was a Chinese girl, so she sat there silently and waited.

"I have been most uneasy, Ming Tai," said her father at length. "Fong Toon brought me news of the police raid last night. I feared that the drug had been discovered and that you might spend the balance of your days in prison."

The fish dealer laughed.

"I am too old at the game, Louie Toy. It was a close call, I confess, but the *ah-peen-yeen* is safely stowed, and I am free to dispose of it."

"It must have been the work of a spy."

"I fear so. As I chatted with a wealthy customer apart from the tables some *ghee* fastened our queues together, and had it not been for the cleverness of my dealers I might be even now in jail. In the confusion, they spirited away a white woman and one of our own people who were under the influence of the drug, along with their layouts. A new sergeant of the Police Devils thought to make a record, but he was disappointed. Two customs inspectors searched the cellar thoroughly, as they thought, but they failed to find even one five-tael tin. They smelled the smoke, they knew that we had violated the law, but the dogs were off the scent. They gave it up at last and we were left to play our games in peace."

"And the new sergeant?"

"He will be removed. One of my agents whispered a word that was passed to police headquarters this morning, along with a certain packet of crisp bills, and assurance has already reached me that the troublesome official will be detailed on an outside beat."

"Good! But Detective Bray and Officer Mulcahey?"

"Officer Mulcahey would sell his soul for a hundred taels, and I am valuable to Detective Bray. He will close his eyes to my misdeeds as long as I continue to give him certain valuable information. An ambitious man can be purchased by other means than the passing of gold coin."

"Your words are music to my ears. The *ah-peen-yeen* is safe. It caused me much concern."

"More than the safety of Ming Tai," sneered Louie's companion. "But you sent for me. Surely more important business than fears for my welfare impelled your message."

"You speak with a serpent's wisdom, Ming Tai. I would question you concerning Luk Chan."

"Luk Chan!"

"Yes; Luk Chan, my enemy. Tell me about him."

There was a slight movement on the balcony above them and the merchant rose quickly, with a warning "S-s-h!"

He went inside his store, ascended to Sen Chee's apartment, opened the door softly, and peered within. His daughter was lying on her couch, head pillowed in her arm, breathing deeply, and she made no movement as he called her name. Silently he pulled the door to and tiptoed down the stairs, seating himself with a grunt of satisfaction before Ming Tai.

"The soul of a conspirator is ever suspicious," he said.

"A conspirator?"

"Yes, for I would conspire against the life of an enemy."

His complacence would have received a rude shock had he known that the lithe figure sprang from its bed at the closing of the door and was even now crouching on the balcony, listening to every word that passed his lips.

"What do you mean?"

"Luk Chan is in love with my daughter."

Ming Tai bit his pipe-stem so violently that the bamboo cracked and splintered between his teeth; but he masked his feelings, and Louie Toy went on.

"Luk Chan makes sheep's-eyes at my Lily Flower. He stands at my windows almost daily and there is a love-sickness in his glare. Sen Chee has noticed him of late and her cheek colors when he looks at her. The sign is ominous; he must be removed."

"You are speaking in riddles, Louie Toy. Come to the point."

"I will, Ming Tai. How much is it worth to remove him?"

"Do you mean murder?"

"It is not a pretty name."

"You dare to talk to me of such a plan!"

"You were not so particular in days gone by. I could remind you of two or three disappearances of our countrymen, when you were poor, and when the bestowing of a few taels were sufficient reward for your work,—work well accomplished, too. I might even mention names, if your memory fails you. For instance, there was the old shoe merchant, Fo—"

"S-s-h!" Ming clutched his wrist in a tremulous grasp. "The past is buried, Louie Toy. Let it sleep."

"Along with your victims," scoffed the merchant.

His visitor crumpled up in his chair, with cheeks gray as a November dawn.

"What do you want of me?" he mumbled. "Let us talk of present business and the sale of *ah-peen-yeen!*"

"No! We will talk of living sacrifices. I will pay you one thousand taels for the life of Luk Chan."

Ming Tai glared at him, his tongue licking parched lips, his fingers trembling.

The merchant could not believe the evidence of his eyes. Ming had never before shown a tremor when a human life hung in the balance of their discussion. But Louie Toy did not know that his own life was forfeit, that the man he thought his ally was playing a double hand and that this sudden new complication, this suggestion coming from the lips of a being already doomed, a suggestion that spelled death to the man chosen by lot to be his slayer, had momentarily unnerved him. It was the Irony of Fate.

But even as Ming Tai cringed there beneath the balcony he was obsessed by a new idea. The deaths of these two members of inimical tongs would remove every obstacle from his path, and he might contrive carefully and lull any lingering suspicion of the merchant by a reluctant acquiescence in his plans.

With an effort he shook off the feeling that possessed him. His beady eyes sparkled and he chuckled as he spread his palms in protest.

"Ming Tai is growing old. The blood courses slowly in his veins. Even his ears have lost their keenness with the years. He will listen more intently to what Louie Toy may propose."

The answer was crisp and biting.

"I will pay you one thousand taels to kill Luk Chan."

Ming sat as if he had not heard, eyes partly closed, countenance immobile.

Louie tapped the arm of his chair impatiently. "One thousand taels, Ming Tai!"

Slowly his auditor raised his head. Slowly he spoke, but there was infinite sarcasm in his tones.

"One thousand taels! Five hundred dollars of the White Devil's money. Has my tong comrade lost his senses? It is a poor night indeed when I do not win more than five hundred dollars from the players in my gambling hall, and that after midnight, Louie, when you are wrapt in peaceful dreams. One thousand taels!! I have been overlong from my customers. It seems that you sent for me but to jest; and I am in no mood for jesting."

He made a movement as if to rise, but Louie Toy leaned over, placed his hand on his shoulder, and thrust him roughly back into his seat.

"In the name of the great Joss, you try my patience. I will pay two thousand taels. Let us plan the details."

"Two thousand devils!!!"

"Two thousand taels, Ming Tai. It is easily earned. The simple snuffing out of a life, a few witnesses cheaply bought, and the affair is ended."

"Remember, I am no longer poor, Louie Toy."

"Three thousand taels, old usurer. It is the price demanded for the sparing of my life by the Bo Sing Tong. Bah! I snap my fingers at them. But I have rated the life of Luk Chan as valuable as my own. I will not raise the price. If your heart has turned you coward, I will find another, who, though cheaper, will yet prove more brave."

Ming Tai pulled the brim of his hat over his eyes.

"What is your plan?" he asked huskily.

A glow of satisfaction thrilled the merchant. He laid a friendly hand upon Ming's knee.

"Start a tong war!" he said abruptly, and felt the limb tremble beneath his palm.

"A tong war?"

"Yes. My life has been threatened by the Bo Sings. You and I are members of the Hop Sing Tong, an organization equally powerful. The gauntlet has been thrown down. Let us take it up. You have great influence in our society. Whisper amongst your confederates that my life is in danger. Arrange a meeting of the tong, mark Luk Chan for slaughter, as a warning to his fellows, and when he is removed get the ear of the Police Devils, as I have already the ear of the Consul; between them they will put a stop to the war, and a long truce will be arranged. It is ever the history of our battles. Besides, Luk Chan is only an humble member of his society and his death will cause but little stir. Come, old comrade, do I not point an easy way?"

Could he have seen the beads of perspiration on Ming Tai's brow, his confidence might have been shaken; but the hat brim masked them while he waited for his answer.

"A tong war is a serious affair, Louie Toy. It is not so easy to arrange as it was in days that are past. The Police Devil's price is high. They are constantly changing. A new chief is to be reckoned with. And the last treaty that was arranged carries a heavy menace to those who break it."

"I am tired of your mouthing! Will you accept my offer, or shall I take my wares to another market?"

"You grow impatient, and I have never failed you. Hold your temper for a little, while I, in turn, make a proposal to you. By its acceptance you will save three thousand taels, your wishes will be gratified, and you may be bound to Ming Tai by ties stronger than those of friendship, Louie Toy."

"What do you mean!!"

"Am I ugly? Am I old? Am I bent and withered by my toil and by the years I have lived?"

"You are babbling nonsense."

"You dodge the question. I will assume that you have answered and that I am all that is hideous, yet I have been your friend."

"Yes! Yes! Go on!"

"I do not want your money, Louie Toy. I want something more precious to me than all your gold, than all the *ah-peen-yeen* that you can buy!—I want your daughter."

Louie Toy gasped, his chin fell, his fingers clutched his chair arms spasmodically. He could not believe the evidence of his ears.

Ming watched him furtively, and several moments passed before he recovered his speech.

"My daughter!! Have you gone insane?—You, you, a creature of the slums, a peddler of fish, the keeper of a gambling-hell, a murderer,—yes, a *murderer!!* You would take my little Sen Chee, my spotless Lily Flower, in your arms! You would caress her with hands stained with the blood of her people! You, the vilest of all vile creeping things, propose this to me! I would rather see her dead than bound to a monster such as you!"

"Fine words, Louie Toy. I might mention names too. Names of more than one who were killed at your bidding. You paid the price. It is admitted. But the slightest whisper breathed in the ears of certain relatives of dead men whose bones have long since been sent back to the Kingdom of Flowers would bring swifter destruction to you, far swifter, than the mandates of the Bo Sing Tong. You reckoned me a fool when I did your bidding. You held me cheap. But I took care that my own hands were not soiled with blood. I had willing tools to do your work. They struck through vengeance, and I have witnesses that will take their oath that you alone killed your enemies.—Louie Toy, the rich, the respected merchant, a friend of the Consul, will become Louie Toy, the murderer of the man who looked with covetous eyes upon the maid he wanted for his own who afterward became the mother of his dear Sen Chee. Do you think I have lived unprepared through all the years? Ming Tai admits he is a great rascal; but he has never been a fool."

The merchant appeared to have aged at least ten years. His arrogance was dispelled, and the fish peddler held a dominant hand. He knew it.

"A worse fate might befall Sen Chee than to become the wife of the rich Ming Tai. Old age ever treats youth and beauty with a lavish hand. Your Lily Flower will be carefully nurtured. She will be decked in jewels and brocaded silks. She will have serving-women to wait upon her and anticipate her every wish. Surely it will please you more than to see her wedded to Luk Chan."

Louie Toy looked at him dully.

"But Sen Chee would never consent!"

"Have you become a woman? Since when have the children of our race disputed their father's will?"

"What is your plan?"

"I have no plan until you consent to my possession of Sen Chee!"

"No! No! No! Ask me anything but that. Take the precious tins of *ah-peen-yeen* in your cellars. Sell them; keep the profit for yourself. Surely that will pay you beyond all reason for the slaying of Luk Chan. The years past have held many ties of affection, but you are at least a score of them older than I, and I am her father. Let us forget the words you have spoken and contrive some other plan."

"Louie Toy, I am in earnest. I am not long for the delights of life. All my wealth will not add to my years. I have tasted the bitterness, now I shall have some of the sweets. You will give me Sen Chee, or I will breathe a tiny whisper that will mean death to you within the week. Come, let us be friends as in the past. A few tears, some broken sighs, a fleeting memory of a hatchet-man who looked at her with desiring eyes; but in a fortnight all will be forgotten, and your Lily Flower will take a childish delight in the pretty baubles bought for her from the coffers of old Ming Tai. Her father will see her daily, he can chide her for her extravagance, he will laugh at her for her treatment of her aged master, and he will—save his life.”

Louie sat in his chair as still as the wooden joss in the meeting-place of his enemies.

At last he looked up with hopeless eyes.

“Ming Tai has a craftier mind than I,” he muttered. “But there is one condition that I demand.”

“And that is?”

“The death of Luk Chan,—my hated enemy!”

“It is a condition that will be swiftly fulfilled.”

“Are you sure that you can handle the Police Devils?”

“Louie Toy has become timorous of a sudden. He has never before failed to have confidence in the cunning of Ming Tai.”

“It is the first time that Ming Tai has failed to demand many golden taels as his reward.”

“My reward is far more precious than your gold, old friend.”

“But, Luk Chan—” hesitantly.

“You need have no fear. Luk Chan will die!”

He bent over to whisper some further details of his plan, but he need not have lowered his voice. The ears of the little maid on the balcony were deaf to all that they might say, for she lay in a huddled heap in her chair, with lips parted and eyes closed, while a last ray of the setting sun gleamed momentarily on her unconscious form.

CHAPTER VI

A DRUG ON THE MARKET

Ming Tai walked back to his fish market in an extremely perturbed frame of mind. He had won a complete victory in his argument with Louie Toy, but the price was heavy. He was committed to a plot to kill Luk Chan, and he feared Luk Chan more than any other hatchet-man in San Francisco.

Louie Toy must, of necessity, die first, or his hand would be shown to the members of the Bo Sing Tong. He had carried water on both shoulders for a long time, but now there was danger of spilling some of it. Should his double-dealing be discovered, he stood a good chance of beating both of these enemies to the Vale of the Thousand Years.

The highbinder is merciless when he discovers treachery in his tong. In fact, it is virtually unknown, so binding is his oath and so deep his reverence for his joss.

Ming was but a passive member of the Hop Sings. He took no part in their meetings, and only to Louie Toy did he ever speak of his membership. He wormed many of their secrets from the merchant and poured them into the ears of Tom Chong.

His craftiness has already been displayed, for he made Detective Bray believe that Luk Chan was a Hop Sing man, with the result that the tong was being carefully watched and his own was allowed more opportunity to carry out its plans.

But the reward would be worth all the danger. He could almost make up his mind to sacrifice Luk Chan and let Sen Chee's father live. Life with the girl would be sweet, but then his treasure-chests would be heavily lined by her father's death, for she was the only living relative. Louie had no cousins even, so far as he could learn.

A tong war would be a serious proposition. When the hatchet-men got to demanding a life for a life and drawing lots for victims no one knew whose turn might be next. He was known to be a miser, he had achieved a certain degree of prominence as keeper of a gambling-house, and his friendship with Tom Chong was no secret.

He counted on the interference of the Police Devils and the wrath of the Chinese Consul. A timely word to Sergeant Bray after his two enemies were disposed of, and hostilities, of necessity, must cease. The police would destroy the josses, would break up the meetings (if the proper tips were given them); then he would give up this scheming and settle down to a life of happiness with his dear Sen Chee. Sen Chee! What a delightful name to conjure with. He rubbed his hands in pleasure and spoke a word in greeting that caused his assistants to stare at him in astonishment as he entered the fish-stall.

He took off his hat, threw it on the littered cover of a crate, and coiled his queue tightly on top of his head.

Then he stripped off his blouse, pulled on a jersey, and wrapping a gunny-sack about his waist, was ready for business.

Customers began to drop in and for an hour or more he was busy weighing fish and bartering with the chattering Celestials.

Along toward eight o'clock he stopped for his frugal meal of rice, hastily disposed of with chop-sticks, and as he pushed back his chair he saw Sergeant Bray crossing the street.

Ming was always ready for a chat with the detective, so he took up his hat and, as he stepped to the sidewalk, put it on his head.

Something was wrong! A bulging object pressed his temple, and he pulled his hat off quickly. In an absent manner he turned down the sweatband and his fingers felt a flat disk nestling inside the brim.

He could not repress a squeal of terror as for the third time he saw the red tiger-cat snarling more hideously than ever. His nerves were completely shattered, his presence of mind was gone.

He gibbered insanely and stared at Sergeant Bray with unseeing eyes as the detective clutched his hand and twisted the poker chip from his fingers.

"What the devil's wrong? Somebody throw a scare into you, Ming?"

The old Chinaman did not answer. He was struggling to regain his wits. He stooped, picked up his hat, turned it over aimlessly, wiped the beads of perspiration from his forehead, and swallowed dryly as he leaned against the door-jamb.

Bray was much interested in the disk. He studied the crude etching, looked over his shoulder, then laid his hand on Ming Tai's arm and shook him roughly.

"Come out of it! I never saw you feazed like this. Where did you get this thing?"

Ming's innate craftiness asserted itself, but it took will-power. His voice was husky as he answered.

"Oh, ketchum in hat, Sargen'. Somebody play jokee."

"That's too thin. This is no joke, Ming. That cat means something."

"No, him not mean nothing. I ketchum piece in till yesterday, I throw him away. Somebody pick him up and drop him in hat maybe."

Ming's voice was under perfect control.

The detective eyed him coldly.

He was grinning in his familiar, guileless way, but deep in his pupils lurked a shadow of fear.

Bray could not be so easily fooled.

"Some highbinder's after your scalp and you know it. Tell me about it. Ain't I your friend?"

"Sure; Sargen' Blay good flen. But me no think highbinder want to hurt Ming Tai. Ming Tai poor man. No use for threaten Ming Tai." The Chinaman's subtlety did not forsake him.

"Poor, hell! I wish I had one-tenth of your dough. Say, Ming, come across! What do you make of it?"

A thought struck the old rascal.

"Maybe Luk Chan he know. Maybe he draw picture of tiger-cat."

"What's Luk Chan got against you?"

Ming appeared to hesitate and looked at his assistants uneasily.

"Come, come! Get it off your chest!"

"Maybe Luk Chan he smuggle *ah-peen-yeen.*"

"What!!!"

"S-s-h! Mustn't talk so loud, Sargen' Blay. You likee ketchum Chinaman smuggle Opium."

"Would I like to 'ketchum'? You bet your life! You put me on to the lay, Ming Tai, and I'll make it worth your while. But what's that got to do with the poker chip?"

"Well, Luk Chan him play fan-tan last night. Him go bloke. When him have no money, he talkee to me one side, he say ketchum dope by San Mateo to-night. Him want me to buy *ah-peen-yeen.*"

"Yes, yes; go on!"

"I tell him no can do; then him get mad. He say keep mouth shut or maybe him kill."

"Ah! Luk Chan sent the chip to frighten you, old man."

"I think so, maybe."

"Well, we'll fix Luk Chan all right. Tell me all you know about this business and leave the game to me. You needn't worry about Luk Chan for the few years you've got to live, if your tip's any good."

"You come back room my shop, Sargen' Blay. This not good pidgin if Luk Chan see you talkee with me."

The detective nodded in assent and accompanied Ming through the darkened stall and into a room in the rear, where he listened to a story that caused his eyes to glisten and elicited several oaths of satisfaction.

The Chinaman's brain was working swiftly. There was a plot to bring in a small lot of opium that night, and Luk Chan was concerned in it. If he could get his enemy stowed safely behind prison bars for a term of years, his plan would be simplified. Sen Chee's lover could not harm him. He did not have overlong to live. Her father would be sacrificed, for, according to the oaths of his tong, another would take up the hatchet-man's task and Louie Toy would not live out the fortnight. His spirits rose as he whispered with the detective.

He unfolded the story of a plan in which he was in reality the chief factor, but he told his tale so cunningly that the slightest suspicion would never be attached to him. He anticipated conditions, and Bray's nerves tingled with the joy of a prospective man-hunt.

He would take care of Ming Tai, and Ming Tai was willing to stand the loss of his share of the drug, if it meant prison for Luk Chan.

Ming's plans were developing rapidly.

A big red motor car chugged impatiently in front of the Harbor Police Station.

Sergeant Bray pulled out his watch.

"It's ten-fifteen," he said. "Pile in, Mulcahey. We ought to make it by eleven. Twenty-five miles to go, and the night's dark. Got your guns, boys?"

He was answered by an affirmative chorus and he swung into a seat in the crowded car.

Besides the policeman, who acted as chauffeur, and Officer Mulcahey there were four picked men from the customs service,—Inspectors Stevens, Head, Lindquist, and Stone.

They carried automatic revolvers and were ready for business. It was an old game for them, and, though the United States Government has long since ceased giving a share of the proceeds of the drug to its men who risk their lives in protecting the revenue, no other thought than the fulfilment of their duty entered their heads.

Despite the darkness they made good time along the bay-shore, and it was but a few moments after eleven o'clock when Detective Bray grasped the driver's arm and the car slowed up.

"We are opposite Monohan's oyster-beds," he said. "The cache can't be more than a quarter of a mile from here. You stick with the machine, Finn, and we'll hike the balance of the way."

"We may need the car damned quick," growled Mulcahey.

Bray ignored him. "When you hear a shot," he continued, "hit the high spots. We'll probably need you."

Silently the inspectors piled out of the automobile, and like shadows six men stole down to the beach. The road wound away from them, but they followed the water's edge, their footsteps making no sound in the wet sand. The stars, shining faintly, made enough light on the rippling waters of the bay for them to see quite a little distance ahead of them.

At last, Bray, in advance, spied the outlines of a shed an hundred yards up the beach.

"That's the place, boys," he whispered. "Let's make the rear of the shack. Thank God, we're on time!"

Separating, they crept away in different directions, and within ten minutes were all huddled together behind the shed.

They whispered, with heads close, for a while, then Lindquist flattened himself on his stomach and crawled stealthily along the wall and disappeared around a corner.

Presently a muffled tap was heard inside. This meant that the coast was clear, and Bray, Mulcahey, and the three inspectors, with less caution, hurried to the front. The door was open and they joined Lindquist inside.

From the dark vantage-point they had gained things were more easily discernible.

Just as the detective was about to speak, Inspector Head clutched his arm.

"What's that on the beach?" he muttered. Straining their eyes, they made out a dim figure huddled on the sand; and as they looked a lantern flashed, momentarily outlining the form, then was hidden from view beneath the man's blouse.

"It's a Chink all right," said Stevens; "I saw his queue."

"The lookout," chuckled Bray. We've got 'em, boys," and he fingered the butt of his gun.

They lay quietly on the floor for at least a quarter of an hour when a sudden sharp intake of Head's breath warned them.

Their eager eyes caught the glint of a light bobbing in the bay and presently they made out the outlines of a Chinese fishing-junk, with its uncouth lug-sail, heading in toward the shore.

The Chinaman on the beach rose, the lantern glimmered from beneath his coat and was swung once, twice, three times, about his head, then quickly doused.

An instant's wait, then a light flashed aboard the junk.

A whispered command and three men sprinted across the sand.

A frightened Mongol felt sinewy arms twist about his waist, but before he could cry out a palm was clapped across his mouth and his lantern was snatched from his hand. Two minutes afterward he was lying on his back in the sand, stripped of his blouse and tightly bound and gagged.

Then the exultant Bray did something the wisdom of which might be open to question. He swung the lantern about his head three times, thrust it beneath his coat and waited.

He cursed impatiently, then smiled as an answering signal came at last from the boat.

He hurried back to the building, hooded the lantern in a corner, and slipped into the Chinaman's blouse. He put on the slouch hat and went back to the water's edge, crouching low on the sand.

But the junk was an interminable time in landing. It hung off shore for a good half-hour.

If the detective's eyes could have penetrated the gloom he might have seen four or five whispering Celestials leaning over the rail and lowering heavily weighted lines. They might have been taking soundings, though such a procedure was unnecessary, for the Chinese fishing-junk is one of the shallowest crafts afloat and is constructed especially for easy grounding on the beach.

The sail flapped idly, but at last it was brought about before a light wind, and the boat crept slowly inshore.

A hundred feet from the beach two barefooted Chinese leaped overboard and, seizing the rail, helped to guide it through the lapping waves until the keel struck softly in the sand.

There was a low hail.

Bray answered it in a reassuring monosyllable and shuffled back a few paces up the beach.

The rest of the boat's crew clambered over the rail and proceeded to business.

A score of boxes were lifted out and deposited on the beach, then, as one of the men turned away and walked toward the shed, the detective whistled shrilly.

Six officers tumbled through the door and tore for the water's edge.

There was a sudden Babel of frightened voices, then a spit of flame as one of the Mongols fired at the leader. Three automatic revolvers cracked; a Chinaman squealed in agony and plunged forward on the sand.

The others, demoralized, were seized before they could put up a fight, and by the time the motor, driven like mad by Finn, chugged to a standstill on the road back of them their arms were bound, two and two together, and they were seated in sullen silence on the beach.

Lanterns were lighted and the inspectors went gleefully to their task.

But somewhere a cog had slipped.

The boxes were overturned, one by one, and their contents dumped out. They were filled with shrimps, and though the tiny shell-fish were pawed about with winnowing fingers, though they were raked figuratively with a fine-tooth comb, there was nothing, absolutely nothing, else in the boxes.

Bray kicked a prostrate Chinaman and questioned him angrily, but elicited only a guttural "No Sabee!"

He flashed his lantern in the faces of the terrified creatures until he singled out one, calmer than the rest, who stared back at him venomously.

He grinned. "Luk Chan! You're the Chink I'm looking for. Where's that dope?"

The tong-man tossed his head.

"Dope! What you mean? We fishermen. Shrimp-fishers. What for you try to kill?"

"None o' that. I'm on to your game. You've got a bunch of *ah-peen-yeen* and I'm after it. Come through, or it will go hard with you. I'll tear your old junk to pieces unless you save me the trouble."

"Better look see. I say we shrimp-fishers. You spoil our catch. What can we do? We poor men. Nobody will pay."

"Aw, we're wasting time, boys. They've got it in the boat. Go to it!"

But although they searched in every nook and cranny of the shallow craft, tore out thwarts, pried up boards, and raked the ballast, there was never a sign of the drug.

They went through the prisoners' clothes, they questioned them, they even gave them a taste of the "third degree," but without avail.

Detective Bray scratched his head and cursed the ancestors of each and every Chinaman that cowered in the sand, but he did not have a leg to stand on, and he knew it.

Ming Tai's name trembled on his lips, he was about to indulge in a special flight of profanity for his particular case when he realized that Luk Chan was eying him stolidly, and he held his tongue.

"Mulcahey, get that fellow in the shed," he commanded.

When the cowering creature was brought before him his story, as much as could be gathered from his "pidgin" English, agreed substantially with what had been told by the rest. They were shrimp-fishers, belated by the wind and tide, and, the night being dark, he had waited on the beach to light his comrades to their landing-place.

Bray knew that there was something amiss, but he did not have the goods.

At last, in disgust, he gave the order to release the prisoners, and their bonds were cut in silence.

The wounded Chinaman had a bullet hole through his arm. He was not badly hurt, and when Officer Mulcahey proposed to take him to the emergency hospital in their machine, he showed a knowledge of English by protesting violently.

They were glad enough not to be burdened with him, and seven very crestfallen men climbed into the automobile, and had very little to say as they were whirred homeward.

When they had vanished around a turn in the road the shrimp-fishers displayed a sudden activity. They piled into the junk, after they had pushed it down the sand, and propelled it swiftly with oars and sail until they were a quarter of a mile from shore.

Then the sail was lowered, an anchor thrown overboard, and several light buoys were hauled in, to which lines were attached. Two men to each line, with considerable grunting, brought a heavy weight to the surface. They felt safe now.

There were a dozen of these weights, large bundles, neatly wrapped in oilskins.

Detective Bray made one fatal mistake when he repeated the signal of the Chinese sentinel.

Luk Chan scented something amiss, and the cargo was temporarily disposed of. At the expense of a few boxes of shrimps, a slightly wounded helper, and a delay of not more than an hour, he landed six hundred five-tael tins of opium on the San Mateo shore.

CHAPTER VII

LUCERO'S WARNING

"Watch Mulcahey!"

Detective Bray turned to his chief, with a look of surprise.

"What's that?"

"I said, 'Watch Mulcahey.'"

"Why, you don't suspect—"

"Yes, I do. There's all kinds of dope been smuggled into Chinatown the last three months, and you haven't caught anybody with the goods. What does it mean? Somebody's tipping them off."

"That might be, Chief. But Mulcahey's square. He's been on the force for three years and his record's clean."

"How did he get that Chinatown detail? Pull!—the boss gave me the program and I couldn't turn him down."

"But he's always been right there with the raids. Why he shot the Chink last night when we pulled off our little fiasco down at San Mateo. Damned if I ain't sore! I sure thought I was going to put one over."

"Yes, and the boys are all laughing at you. Those Chinamen were not shrimpers. It's a cinch, Bray, that some one put 'em wise."

"Anyway, I think you are wrong about Mulcahey, Chief."

"Well, I don't! You know he's got the fattest beat in Chinatown and that all the hop-heads are hitting the pipe. In the last two weeks the price of dope has dropped at least one-quarter. Now what does that mean?"

"It means that there's lots of it on the market."

"Sure it does. Can you depend on Ming Tai?"

"I feel certain that he is square. He gave me that information about Luk Chan and the Hop Sings digging up the hatchet, and everything points to a tong war."

"Well, something's wrong. I've been in this business for twenty-seven years and I wouldn't have got to my present position without considerable knowledge of men. You know I don't object to a lot of this graft. It's necessary. You fellows are entitled to some pickings. But, by God, when you go up against the United States Government it's a different story! Wouldn't it be a nice state of affairs if some of these Customs Inspectors got the goods on one of my coppers and put him over for smuggling? Why, we'd have to tie the old city up tighter than a drum. Now you get at the bottom of this damn quick."

"But what makes you think that Mulcahey—"

"I'll tell you. I saw a little item in the 'Real Estate Transfers' last week that set me to thinking. I had it followed up, and found that Mul had bought two lots out in Sunset. He paid cash, too; three thousand dollars." The detective whistled. "Mul hasn't saved three thousand dollars or three thousand cents out of his salary as a patrolman, that's a safe bet. I don't mind him sticking up a faro-bank or getting some saloon graft once in a while, but I won't stand for a hop deal."

"But the boss? He's a mighty good friend of yours, and he's behind Mulcahey."

"I don't give a damn. He'll drop him like a hot potato if we catch him with the goods. Now, Bray, you've been square, that's why you are a poor man, and I depend on you. Keep your eye on Mulcahey, and let me know the minute you spot anything."

Chief Marvin turned to his desk and picked up a letter.

Bray looked at him a moment, shook his head doubtfully, then lit a cigar and went out into the street.

It was close to noon, but he thought he would stroll up to Chinatown and give Ming Tai a grilling before dinner. Besides, Officer Mulcahey went on duty at twelve o'clock.

Just as he turned into Fish Alley he saw Luk Chan coming toward him. He dodged into a doorway, and when the Chinaman had passed he slipped out and followed him.

If he had been a trifle more wary he might have noticed a small Celestial near the fish market, who started slightly when he saw him and who immediately dogged his footsteps in turn.

Luk Chan crossed Dupont street, looked into a Window at the corner, walked leisurely across Clay, and read the bulletins displayed there, for five minutes or more. The detective hovered in the background and the Mongol, shadowing him, stepped into a hallway and fumbled beneath his blouse, producing a piece of soiled paper, which he concealed in his hand.

At last Luk Chan walked leisurely up Clay street, turning into Waverly Place. The other Chinaman took a short cut through the hallway and darted out of a back entrance just in time to see him enter a lodging-house across the alley. Bray had not yet turned the corner.

Luk Chan walked down a long corridor and, as he placed his foot on the lowest step of a narrow stairway, something whirred through the air and lifted his hat from his head. It fell with a soft spat on the stairs, and as he turned with a cry of alarm, a revolver slipped from his sleeve and his fingers tightened on its butt.

The hall was empty.

Stooping, he picked up his hat and bounded up the stairs.

At a turn in the corner a gas-jet flared. His eyes widened as he stared at his hat crown. Piercing it was a slender stiletto, with a blade fully nine inches long and a mother-of-pearl handle. He drew it out, trembling slightly, and a twisted piece of paper close to the hilt rustled in his palm. Wondering, he smoothed it against the wall and by the flickering gaslight read five scrawled words in English, *"Beware; Bray is following you."*

He was mystified. But he had not time for the solving of riddles.

Action was the thing.

He extinguished the light and ran to the end of the hall. He tapped on a door and when it was opened darted inside and locked it after him. He muttered a brief sentence to the astonished inmate, then threw up the window and climbed out onto the fire-escape. He looked about him, but fortunately Stockton street was deserted. He swung over the railing, made a ten foot drop, and hurried up the sidewalk to Sacramento. He strolled down the hill, greeting several friends on the way, went up Dupont to California, passed St. Mary's Cathedral, and stepped into a vacant lot next to it, back of a broken wall of a building that had never been razed since the earthquake.

A wooden fence, used as a bill-board, masked its ugliness.

A furtive glance over his shoulder, then he crawled under it and dived beneath the sidewalk. There he found standing space and a brick wall with an iron door.

He fitted a key to the lock, the door clanged behind him, and he waited in darkness.

A half-hour passed.

Crouched on the floor, his limbs were cramping from inaction, when there was a sudden creaking of a lock, a flash of light, and darkness again.

He heard the heavy breathing of the intruder, but he remained motionless.

An electric torch flooded the cubby-hole with its ray and Officer Mulcahey swore at him.

"Why the hell didn't you say something. I've been watching for you for fifteen minutes. I thought your foot had slipped."

Luk Chan stood up.

"I was followed," he said simply.

"The devil you say! Who was it?"

"Sergeant Bray. I threw him off my trail, but I came before the appointed time."

(The Chinaman had been educated in the American schools and did not attempt the subterfuge of "pidgin" English with Officer Mulcahey. Business was too pressing.)

They were in a small octagonal room, with a low ceiling, one side of which was piled high with wooden boxes, over the topmost of which showed the upper edge of a closed door. The place was weird and suggestive of spooks.

They stood below the steeple of St. Mary's Cathedral, and the little storeroom had no doubt long ago been abandoned and its existence forgotten by the changing sextons.

Officer Mulcahey took off his helmet and crossed himself.

"'Tis a great place for the dope. Safely hidden in the bosom of Mother Church! Sure and it seems like sacrilege."

But he made quick peace with his conscience by the act of veneration, and turned to business.

"You've got a hell of a lot of it, Luk Chan. Do you think Bray is on?"

"No. He followed me because he saw me at the fishing-junk last night. Why did you shoot Tom Ming?"

"Faith and I couldn't help it. Didn't I have to make good. I only winged him anyway. I didn't shoot to kill."

"True."

"Well, lave it go at that. How about my divvy?"

Luk Chan stepped toward the boxes, laid his hand on one of them, and began to count slowly in Chinese.

The policeman mopped his brow. The place was stuffy.

At last the tong-man spoke.

"There are twenty boxes of *ah-peen-yeen*,—a little over eight hundred pounds. They will sell for at least twelve thousand dollars in your money."

"Whew! That sounds good."

"If we are not disturbed they will be sold in two weeks. I said, 'If we are not disturbed.'"

Mulcahey nodded. "I understand. Ye'll not be disturbed if I live out the two weeks. But how about my end of it?"

"Ten per cent. That is our agreement."

"Sure, twelve hundred dollars. I'm itchin' to get my hands on it."

The Chinaman's lip curled. He held an utter contempt for this creature that circumstances made it necessary for him to deal with.

"How do I know that you will play fair? It's a lot of money and something might happen to you. God help you if you throw me down. I'll put the chief on and he'll raid every joint in Chinatown. They can't connect me with it. Nobody would believe a Chink under oath."

Luk Chan straightened, his fingers caressed the revolver-butt, and for an instant murder gleamed in his eye. But he conquered the impulse and looked steadily at Mulcahey.

"Have you ever known one of my race to break his word?"

Mulcahey dropped his eyes and shifted sheepishly as he pushed back his helmet.

"Oh, that's all right, but I can use that money."

"Will you take a thousand dollars as your share, in cash?"

"Sure! In a minute."

Without a word, Luk Chan fumbled at the bosom of his blouse and drew out a roll of bills. He stepped in front of the policeman, and counting out ten one-hundred-dollar greenbacks, thrust them into his hand.

"You see we trust you, even if you are not of our race," he said simply.

The policeman, ashamed, mumbled an apology. "You're white all right, Luk Chan. Sure, and I did you an injustice. I hope you don't have no trouble gettin' rid of the hop. Leave it to me to give you the tip if any of the boys get to nosin' around. Say; I'm leery of the chief. He's a wise un, and we've got to fix it up pretty quick to pull a layout, or he'll be asking questions. Can't we cook up something with Ming Tai? Ain't there some Chink who ain't got any friends that we can catch with a bunch of dope? Ming's all right; he'll stand in."

"I am not sure. I fail to understand the raid last night. Ming Tai was the only man outside of my companions who knew the *ah-peen-yeen* was to be brought ashore. How did Detective Bray learn our secret? If Ming Tai told him, he is a traitor. If Ming Tai was playing a game on him, he would have warned me. It was a close call. If I had not been suspicious of the second signal of the lantern I would, even now, be on the road to your prison."

"Gee, but you're a smart Chink, Luk Chan! I've got to hand it to you. You can talk better 'American' than lots of our coppers. Why ain't you in some better business than smuggling dope?"

The hatchet-man smiled. "In the eyes of my people, I do no wrong. Your people make laws for themselves. The Chinaman's customs are sacred to him, and they interfere with them. He goes his own way, he rights his wrongs, he does not ask for help from you. We are a separate community. Do you know of a white man who has ever suffered at our hands?"

"No, I don't. But say; I've got to get out of here. If the sergeant misses me from my beat, I'll go on the carpet sure. What the devil was that!"

Luk Chan snatched the electric torch from his hand and the room was plunged in darkness.

The policeman's knees sagged beneath him. He dropped to the floor with a whimper of fear that was stilled as he felt his companion's fingers sink into the fleshy part of his arm.

They crouched there in tense silence, and after an interval their straining ears heard a gentle scratching on the door.

"My God! my God!" mumbled the white man, but the yellow one clutched his revolver and crawled stealthily to the panel. He pressed his ear against it and listened. A half-dozen times, at intervals, the scratching was repeated, but he was motionless.

At last a muffled whisper came to him, "Luk Chan, Luk Chan; *amigo,* a friend."

Where had he heard that voice before? The tone was familiar, but he was baffled. Again it came a little louder, "*Amigo,* Luk Chan, *amigo.*"

His memory groped for the key, then, of a sudden, he had it.

He fumbled for a moment with the lock, opened the door softly, jerked a small figure into the room, and pressed the button of his electric torch.

Juan Lucero cowered on the floor before them, and Mulcahey stared at him, jaw hanging, hair disheveled, so distraught by fear that he forgot that he was armed and might easily kill both the inmates of his hiding-place and make a clean get-away, had he so minded.

Luk Chan turned to him.

"Get up!" he commanded, and there was a world of infinite scorn in his tone.

The policeman stumbled to his feet, found his helmet, and leaned weakly against the wall.

The tong-man took a pearl-handled stiletto from his girdle and handed it to the boy on the floor.

"This is yours," he said. "There is a bond of gratitude between us. You need have no fear. I am your friend,—your *amigo.* Why did you follow me here?"

The boy caught his wrist and rose slowly.

"Oh, *si;* yes, yes. The man of the police follow you. Señor Bray he walk where you walk, but he not see Juan Lucero. I am afraid, and I throw knife to warn you, me, Juan Lucero, the great Lucero; I throw the dagger at the Hippodrome, I make the money for my *mujercita,* my Carlotta, I tell—"

"Aw, cut it out," snapped Mulcahey irritably. "What the devil do you mean sneakin' after me like this? I'll put you in the jug, I'll—"

Luk Chan raised his hand and something in his eyes commanded obedience.

"Leave this boy to me. You are a fool. Don't you know that he has saved your star, your life perhaps? Go on, *amigo.*"

Juan looked at him gratefully.

"After I throw the knife I run quickly to the corner. I see you, you come down the hill, you go past the Cathedral,"—he crossed himself,—"you vanish—so,"—snapping his fingers,—"behind the wall. I wait. Pretty queeck Señor Bray he come along. He look like maybe he lost something. But he cannot find. I hide behind the church. Then this *hombre,* he come too. He go behind the wall where you go. Señor Bray he gone by that time, he not see him. But I wait—wait—wait for long time, and you not come. I think maybe you are kill and little Chinese girl she be sorry, maybe and *manana* she cry—"

Luk Chan interrupted him.

"How did you find the door?"

"Well, pretty soon I am excited and I go behind the wall. I find hole in sidewalk and I queeck crawl in, then I scratch the door, I think maybe I can help. I have one knife more, and I not want little Chinese girl to cry."

The tong-man turned to Mulcahey.

"You see the boy has a heart of gold," he said.

"The murderin' greaser would have slipped a knife into my ribs."

"I think he would," drily.

"But what are we going to do with him? He'll give the snap away. If Bray gets hold of him I'm gone."

"You can leave him to me. He owes a debt of gratitude to one of my race. He will not forget it."

"*Si! Si!*" mumbled Juan. "But I almost do forget. I come to look for you when I see Señor Bray. I must let you know or you will be keel."

"What do you mean?"

"Ming Tai! You think him *amigo*. You make mistake. Ming Tai is *malo hombre,* he is one bad man. He will hire you to be keeled. I know; I hear. Ming Tai makes the plot against your life."

"How do you know?"

The boy dropped to his feet, sobbing as he buried his face in his hands.

"No! No! No! I must not tell. You must not ask me. But I know. *I know.* I tell you I hear. They promise that you be keel."

Luk Chan stood like a statue, but beyond the dilating of his nostrils he showed no sign of emotion.

Officer Mulcahey swore suddenly.

"Damn your soul; you will tell! We'll put him through the third degree. What do you think, Luk Chan? If Chief Marvin gets him in the sweat box he'll come through all right."

The Chinaman eyed him for an instant.

"Are you insane? You forget that your own hands are soiled."

"Ah, he won't dare to squeal on me. Nobody'd believe him. There ain't nobody got nothin' on me."

"You are mistaken! If you arrest the boy, your chief will learn that you are a smuggler of opium."

"Who'll tell him?"

"I will."

"What!!"

"I mean what I say. There is a blood-bond between Juan Lucero and Luk Chan. The Oriental does not reward the saving of his life with treachery. If Chief Marvin sees this cache of *ah-peen-yeen*, Officer Mulcahcy himself may get a taste of the third degree. You have your pay in advance. It is the price of the sealing of your eyes and ears. And do not take my warning lightly."

The policeman shifted uneasily.

"But what the h—l am I going to do?"

"Go back to your beat and leave the boy to me."

CHAPTER VIII

PERFUME OF LILIES

Sen Chee lay on her couch.

It was midafternoon and she had stolen upstairs after an hour of vain watching for Luk Chan. She said nothing to her father and, though he noticed her as she left the counter, he forbore questioning her. She had been drooping of late and he thought he knew the reason of it. But he had worries of his own. He dreaded the hour when Ming Tai would claim his daughter, but the affair had been taken out of his hands. The old fish dealer had proven his master.

Well, Sen Chee was but a child. She would have a rich husband and he had enough of the world's goods to live in Peking for the balance of his days. He would be a mandarin, wealthy and respected, and Sen Chee—bah! he would forget. There were things well forgotten. He could not remain in San Francisco alone. The girl had been his one comfort in life. A haunting memory, a memory of a young Celestial who had loved her mother and who had disappeared mysteriously many years ago, was ever with him.

True, it had faded. He had dwelt in security, had amassed many taels and become a power in Chinatown. But it had returned with added poignancy with the threat of Ming Tai.

He would wait until the affair was settled, then he would dispose of his business and doze away his days in the land of his fathers.

The girl tossed restlessly.

A dull pain had lingered in her bosom ever since she had heard the plot against her lover. She knew not how to warn him. She had no idea where he might be found. There was no one in the world she could trust. Wait! The Mexican boy whom her father had befriended! He had often looked at her with imploring eyes, the eyes of a dog wishing to show its gratitude but denied the power of speech. Then she knew that he had had something to do with

Luk Chan's escape from her balcony, and he had kept her secret. She thought he was in her father's packing-room but she did not dare to go to him.

The act would be questioned.

The superstition of her race mastered her. A name danced in her memory. A sudden thrill of hope attended it.

Him Yick Jan. Him Yick Jan, the herb-doctor, the teller of fortunes. A dignitary greatly respected by San Francisco's Celestial population. He had cured many diseases of the body and mind. His prophecies were traditions amongst the Chinese maidens; and, though the daughters of the upper classes do not mingle so freely as do their American sisters, though there is much more of restraint in their communion, certain secrets are whispered, and tales of potent love-philters dispensed by the old doctor had reached her ears.

A slight color flushed her cheeks.

She rose and changed quickly to her street costume; then descended the stairs and walked boldly past her father, his eyes widening as she left his store.

Many of the Chinamen stared at her as she passed them on the walk, but she was unaware of their glances.

Opposite the market of Ming Tai she hesitated for a moment as she saw the old fish dealer smoking his pipe in the sun. But it was too late, he had seen her. Dropping her eyes, she walked to the plaza, turning into the little street at its eastern end, and halting before a house built in the Oriental style, with gilded cupolas and gaudily painted balconies hung with Chinese lanterns, over the door of which were many scrawling characters in her native tongue.

Ming Tai's pipe was suddenly neglected. He hurried to the corner, peered stealthily about an angle of the wall until he saw the girl stop at the herb-doctor's door.

Then intuition seized him and he scuttled back to Fish Alley. Passing his store, he trotted along the little street to a narrow entrance about midway of the block and dived inside.

In a room heavily draped with Oriental hangings, a very old man, garbed in mandarin robes, bent over a table. He had a knife in his hand, and with its blade was crumbling into a fine powder tiny bits of a substance resembling chalk, which he was depositing in little glass vials. As each was filled he moistened a colored label and wrapped it deftly around the bottle. Along one side of the room was a row of shelves filled with jars containing herbs and medicines, many of which are beyond our Caucasian ken.

Some of them held *ginseng*, the precious root so venerated by all Chinese, whose value is determined by its resemblance, or fancied resemblance, to the human form. The nearer it attains perfection, the higher is its price; and the best pieces are shipped from China wrapped in cotton wool and packed more carefully than the most fragile articles of Satsuma or Cloisonne ware.

There was Sesamun seed, from which a powerful oil is made. There were dried lizards, flattened out against the sides of their jars in loathsome hideousness; bean-sticks; Narcissus root, Caladium bulbs; tiger's-teeth, which, when ground to powder, were supposed to instil ferocious fighting power in the bosoms of the tong-men; tiny cuttle fish; ground taros; sliced pumelos; loongan, the preserved meat of the lychee nut; water-chestnuts; herbs and powders innumerable; pills of gigantic size and indescribable hue; water-snakes, preserved in alcohol; spiders even, and little brown water-dogs, with yellow bellies upturned.

The place was creepy, and, though the sun was shining, its shades were tightly drawn, and Him Yick Jan worked beneath a green-shaded gas-lamp.

The old doctor mumbled indistinguishable phrases in a cracked voice as he mixed the powder and stopped at frequent intervals to adjust the absurd horn-rimmed spectacles that threatened constantly to fall off his nose. He was old, older than Ming Tai, older than the oldest denizen of Chinatown; but an easy living and his knowledge of medicine had kept his faculties alert. His scanty hair was white,—there was a scraggly tuft on his chin, a tenuous wisp on his lip, and his queue, braided tightly, hung like a rat's tail from beneath his mandarin cap, in the coral button of which was set a large pearl.

There remained but two or three of the vials to be filled when the jangling of a bell caused him to raise his head and blink solemnly. He seemed loath to move. He was imperturbable, beyond starting; but this was the call of business. It meant a tael or two in his coffers. His avarice had grown with years of hoarding. Slowly he shuffled to the door and entered a dim waiting room. Opening its door in turn, he ushered in a timid Chinese maid, who, at his command, seated herself nervously on the edge of an ebony stool.

Before he could question her he heard another summons. A short, whirring buzz in the laboratory where he had been working.

Excusing himself he left his visitor, crossed the room, and went into a hallway. He admitted another Chinaman at a rear entrance,—an old man, too,—who whispered to him in an eager tone.

What he said roused the old doctor to action. He nodded briskly, rubbed his palms together, and at last led the newcomer into the room of the jars. He laid his finger on his lips, then went back to the girl.

She had never seen Him Yick Jan. He had never laid eyes on her, yet his first words filled her with a superstitious awe.

"Why has the daughter of Louie Toy come to consult me?"

He knew her! This reader of the future must be all-powerful. He might tell her what she wished to know; aye, more even.

She shivered, but did not answer.

"What is your ailment, little Sen Chee? I have drugs for them all."

She continued to stare at him mutely, and at last he bent over, taking a wrist in either hand and pressing knotted fingers on her pulses, which throbbed with presentiment.

He was silent for a full minute, peering at her with gimlet eyes that looked uncanny behind his quaint spectacles. She felt that he was reading her soul secrets and she shrank beneath his gaze, but he spoke soothingly.

"It is a heart ailment, little Sen Chee, but it is not beyond curing. Your pulses tell me that your bosom is disturbed, that distressing tremors thrill you. Is it not so?"

She raised her head appealingly. Still clasping her wrists, he commanded her with his eyes.

"Is it not so, Lily Flower?"

Her answer was an almost imperceptible nod, and he went on:

"Do you seek forgetfulness? A tiny vial of powdered lotus root will remove all unpleasant memories of the past and bring dreams of a happy future. It will banish unpleasant thoughts; you will forget the lover that has proved untrue, you will cease to remember the existence of—Luk Chan!"

With a cry of alarm, she jerked her hands from his grasp and half rose, but he laid his palm on her shoulders and forced her gently back upon her seat.

"Do not be alarmed, Sen Chee. Him Yick Jan knows the world's secrets. His old eyes peer behind the veil. He is all-powerful. With potent herbs, he holds the mastery of Life itself. Would you destroy an enemy, possess the heart of a lover, or read the story of your future years, you have but to whisper your wishes and to pay my fee. Your confidences will go with me to the vale of Death. But your happiness may be assured. Come, shall I mix a powder of some potent drug to dull your sorrow, or shall I unfold the chart of futurity to your eyes?"

She looked at him timorously, but he raised his hand and smiled.

"Your eyes tell me," seductively, again holding her hand.

"Sen Chee would know if love attends the days to come. Her heart is young, it cries out for a mate. I will fetch the stone."

He glided away, closing the door noiselessly behind him, and she sat in a daze until his return.

He lighted a lamp with a rose-colored globe of ground glass and laid a small block of mottled onyx on the stand beside it.

"Come closer, little daughter," he commanded, "and we will consult the oracle."

Impelled by some strange influence that he possessed, and soothed by the lamp's soft ray, she slowly rose and moved to his side, bending over, as with a trembling finger he traced imaginary outlines on the stone.

"I see a tong-man's head," he murmured. "Look! There is the outline of the forehead and the nose." Then he rubbed his palm over the smooth surface with an impatient gesture.

"But there is a cloud across it." He traced the lines again. "Ever the cloud! It portends evil" She shuddered.

"Be patient, child. I see no evil for thee."

He mumbled low and moved his forefinger about the onyx block in indecisive hesitance.

At last he ceased abruptly.

"The tong-man vanishes, Sen Chee. You will not see him again!"

Her breath came in a short gasp of anxiety.

"Do not sorrow, Lily Flower. The lamp shows a rose-tinted future."

He traced rapidly again.

"I see another man, an older one. A man of wealth. And the outlines of a woman's head stand out closely. See, Sen Chee. The face is your own. It is dim to you but plain to my accustomed eyes. I see your husband, Sen Chee. Not the tong-man that your fancy dwells on, not the lover that you think is true, but another, more worthy, who will make you happy through the years."

She clutched his arm.

"But Luk Chan, does he live?"

"He lives, Sen Chee. But he is faithless. He has forgotten the little maid who fell a victim to his desiring eyes. Even now his plans are laid. He will abandon her without a parting thought. He sails for the Kingdom of Flowers on the great black steamer within the fortnight,—and he takes a wife with him."

He felt her hand tremble beneath his shoulder and a twinge of remorse seized him, but it was quickly forsaken.

"No, no! The stone lies. Tell me that it is in not true!"

"It is the truth, Sen Chee. The sacred stone is infallible. But you will soon forget. I see a happy future."

She swayed and he rose quickly, helping her to her seat.

"Shall I prepare the drug that will bring forgetfulness?" he questioned.

She shook her head and he stood before her, waiting.

At last she forced her wits to action, fumbled in a tiny silken bag that hung from her wrist and, producing a coin, pressed it in his palm.

He spoke to her unctuously, but she rose, of a sudden, and before he could interfere hurried to the door and slipped out into the hall.

He smiled, then turned away and entered his laboratory.

Ming Tai sprang from his chair and questioned him eagerly.

"It was well that I was forewarned," he answered. "Louie Toy's daughter carries a heavy heart to her home."

They whispered together for a time and Ming interrupted him frequently with low chuckles of pleasure.

When the tale was ended the old fish dealer departed in high glee, and Him Yick Jan caressed a gold coin lovingly as he turned to the refilling of his vials.

Instinct alone guided Sen Chee back to her father's store. Her eyes noted never a passer-by, but constantly before them danced the vision of an old fortune-teller and a fateful stone. When she reached the Canton Bazaar she hurried to her room and sobbed out her agony on her silken pillows.

Hours passed, and she was roused at last by a summons to her evening meal. Mechanically she partook of food and, when she had finished, sought her couch again.

The evening waned, the old clock in the Cathedral tower struck nine, and its last reverberating peal roused her.

A plan that had been hovering in her mind took sudden form, and she sat up on the edge of the bed. It was a sin, one of the most unpardonable sins of her race.

It meant soul-punishment for a thousand years. A thousand years her soul would writhe in torture, but it would be purged at last. What were a thousand years in the reckoning of Eternity? What were a thousand years of soul-torment to the bodily suffering of the present, the living ages of hideous heart-pain? Luk Chan was faithless,—Luk Chan, who had whispered vows that shattered all the defenses of her love. This was more than she could stand.

Quickly she ran to her windows, closed them and fastened them, but, for some unknown reason, she forgot to lock her door. It was closed, and being distraught, she thought, no doubt, the bolt was thrown.

A gas-fixture, with three jets, depended from the ceiling, directly over her bed.

She stood for a while, staring into vacancy. Her apartment was distant from the sleeping chamber of her father. She would be undisturbed.

The store would not be closed until midnight. Long before that hour she would be past all human aid.

A light, despairing sob, then she reached upward and opened the cocks, throwing herself on her couch as the poisonous gas escaped through its vents.

Its odor assailed her nostrils, it was disagreeable at first, but after several minutes had passed she failed to notice it. Her head seemed lighter, her heart throbbed madly, she rose and fell on little billowy waves, strange thoughts danced through her brain. Thoughts of Luk Chan, of his strong arms embracing her closely, of the evening on her balcony when she had hidden him behind her chair.

Her heart beat faster and faster, distantly she heard the old clock chime the half-hour. Why, it was not hard, this slipping into the Vale of the Thousand Years. What was the strange perfume that she breathed? Was it the scent of lilies? Yes; that was it. The fragrance of the crushed blossom that she had given Luk Chan. He stood before her, the faded petals were hidden beneath his blouse; he leaned over, she pressed her face against his bosom and drew a deep inhalation of its incense. Something throbbed like a trip-hammer in her temples; the world rolled out from under her; she felt herself falling, falling, falling through space; her lips parted, she tried to call her lover's name, but failed; a little broken sigh; then oblivion draped her with the shadow of Eternity.

Luk Chan sat in the darkness in a lodging-house in Waverly place. There was a price on his head, but he took no thought of his danger. Sen Chee's image thrilled him. He longed to clasp her in his arms, to fly with her to some foreign country where the vengeance of his tong could not reach him.

His blood-oath commanded her father's death. Was there no way out of it? His chin sank on his bosom, a faint perfume was wafted to his nostrils. He drew a faded Narcissus blossom from his blouse and pressed his face close against his palms.

The call of the lily was insistent.

His mind was made up, he would visit Sen Chee's balcony.

Thrusting the token back into its resting-place, he went out into the night.

Just before he reached the joss-house he recognized a skulking Chinese figure and spoke sharply.

It was the Mexican, Juan Lucero, and together they went into the building.

The temple was deserted and they passed through it quickly. Climbing the stairs to a narrow attic, they mounted a ladder and crawled through an open scuttle onto the roof.

Luk Chan laughed as he saw a bamboo pole lying close against the coping, where he had left it after his first visit.

He peered over the edge. The balcony was deserted.

Muttering some low directions to Lucero, he lowered the pole until it rested beneath Sen Chee's casement.

The Mexican steadied it as he slid downward, then drew it up and waited on guard.

CHAPTER IX

A Running Fight

Luk Chan listened at Sen Chee's window for a while, then he tapped lightly on the pane. He drew back, flattening himself against the wall, but several minutes passed and his signal was not answered. The night was dark. There was no moon, and but a dim starlight. Still, he could discern the outlines of near-by objects. He could see the majolica flower-pots on their rail, and the scent of the nodding lilies soothed him. He would be patient. Perhaps his sweetheart was still in her father's store. He looked up, and thought he saw Lucero's head above the coping of the joss-house wall.

He whispered a low sentence of warning and the head disappeared. At last he went to the window again and tapped more loudly. All was silence. He grew uneasy. A feeling of disappointment seized him. Somehow he had imagined that the girl waited nightly on her balcony for him, and his vanity had a fall.

The curtains were partly drawn, and he shook the window, softly calling her name. Then he lowered his head, trying to peer through the panes. He pressed his face close to the glass but his eyes could not penetrate the blackness.

A sudden determination seized him and, stealthily, he tried to raise the frame. He would slip into her chamber and leave some token on her pillow that would tell of his visit. Perhaps she would be sorry that she had not watched for him; perhaps not. The heart of a lover ever sees the evil side. Perhaps she had forgotten him. Well, his visit would not be repeated. He had risked his life to come to her, and she either slept soundly or waited for belated customers in her father's store. It was no place for her. She should be in her chamber. What if she *were* there? She might waken and cry out in her fright before she recognized her visitor. It was a foolish thought. He would go back to the joss-house and send a message by Lucero. Another night she might condescend to take the air on her balcony.

He turned to the rail, but some impelling force mastered him and, with a low exclamation, he wheeled to the window again and, drawing a clasp-knife

71

from his pocket, worked its blade through the slit between the frame, in an endeavor to spring the catch.

He fumbled with it unsuccessfully for a time, then stopped all of a sudden. His nostrils had caught the scent of escaping gas as he held his face close to the crack.

A hideous fear seized him.

Could it be possible that there had been an accident? No; surely Sen Chee was not in her chamber. But his great love swept caution away on a wave of anxiety.

He drew his revolver and struck its butt sharply on the window pane. As the broken glass fell in tinkling bits upon the sill a poisonous vapor poured out through the opening.

He thrust his hand through the jagged hole, taking no heed of a gashed wrist, unfastened the catch, and threw up the window. He sprang inside, knocking over a chair and striking his knees against the foot of Sen Chee's couch, while his head swam from the noxious inhalation. He stretched out a trembling hand and felt the girl's limp form. Throwing his arms around her, he lifted her and staggered to the sill.

When he had borne her into the air he deposited her tenderly on the little wicker seat in one corner of the balcony and leaned over, breathing her name in fierce whispers and calling on his Joss to bring her back to life. He chafed her hands and slapped her wrists, tore her blouse loose at the bosom, even opened her lips and pressed his own close to them in a frantic endeavor to force breath into her lungs. But she lay limp in the starlight, and his heart was bursting with despair. Her arms fell as he released them and her fingers trailed lifelessly on the balcony floor. A sob broke from the tong-man's lips. Tears filled his eyes. He had never known fear. He had faced his enemies. A price had been set upon his head in the last highbinder war, but this was the first time in all his life that he had shed a tear.

She had gone to the Vale of the Thousand Years. She had destroyed her body and her soul. She was braver, far braver than he. A despairing thought struck him. He could join her. Her father would be spared, for a time at least, and he could dwell, blood-guiltless, with his loved one through the thousand years of soul-torment.

He picked up his revolver. He had dropped it beneath the window when he broke the pane.

He mumbled a brief incantation to his Joss, bent over and laid his head on Sen Chee's bosom, and pressed the muzzle against his side.

The hammer cocked itself slowly under the pressure of his finger, then suddenly the gun was hurled to one side and he leaped to his feet, lifting the girl roughly in his arms.

As he faltered there on the borderland of Eternity his ear, pressed against her breast, had heard a faint pulsation of the heart that told him that his dear Sen Chee still lived.

He shook her roughly, then threw her back into the chair and snatched her from it again; he seized her arms and raised them above her head, pumping them up and down.

He implored her to come back to him, he called her all the endearing names in the Chinese tongue. He cast caution to the winds and took no thought of the loudness of his tones. He even cried out in happiness as he felt a flicker of breath against his face while he bent eagerly over her.

Exultantly he snatched her to him and held her close, striding up and down the little balcony and swinging her from side to side, crooning to her as if she were an infant in his strong arms.

At last his straining eyes, burning above her closed ones, saw an almost imperceptible flutter of her lashes, and hope restored his scattered senses. He carried her to her chair once more, lowered her carefully into it, and dropped to his knees beside her, holding her hands tightly as he bent over her pallid face.

At last he had his reward, for her lids opened slowly; but the eyes that looked into his were vacant and unseeing. She closed them again and her bosom rose and fell as her lips parted in a tremulous sigh. The suspiration was music to Luk Chan's soul. He was content. His prayer had been answered. Through all the years to come nothing would ever convince him that she had not passed beyond the vale, and that his great love and his fervent prayers to his Joss were not the sole agents of her return.

He pressed his lips against her ear and whispered her name. Again and again he called her and at last her subconsciousness responded to the potency of his will.

Her eyes opened once more and this time they flickered with the light of sanity.

She looked at him for what seemed aeons to Luk Chan and the dear eyes widened and widened.

At last partial understanding came to her and, brokenly, she breathed his name.

One of our race would have smothered his sweetheart in frenzied caresses, but Luk Chan simply looked at her with joy-beaming eyes. Slowly she lifted an arm and laid it on his shoulder, drawing him close to her.

She was so dazed, so stupefied by the poisonous gases that had filled her lungs, that, beyond that first happy murmur, she was content to lie speechless, content to know that the old herb-doctor had spoken with a false tongue and that her lover was restored to her.

A sharp crunch of broken glass, and Luk Chan turned his head in alarm. Standing just outside her window was Sen Chee's father, stunned, momentarily, by the vision he beheld.

But even as the tong-man attempted to rise Louie Toy leaped upon him and vengeful fingers were twined about his throat.

They struggled on the balcony floor.

Luk Chan was the more powerful of the two, but he was at a disadvantage. The girl moaned and tried to rise, but she was too weak and fell back limply in her chair.

As her lover twisted his body in an attempt to shake off the strangling clutch he swung one arm backward and his fingers struck some cold object on the floor. He thrilled with the contact and gripped it avidly. It was his revolver, forgotten since the breaking of the window pane.

He caught the muzzle firmly and with a mighty effort struggled to his feet. He swung it upward in a gleaming half-circle. Too late Louie Toy saw the descending pistol-butt. With a cry of fear he tried to jerk his head away, but it struck him full on the temple. His grip on his enemy's throat relaxed; he swayed for a brief instant, then slipped in a huddled heap to the floor.

Luk Chan called the Mexican's name, but there was no answer. He called again louder. Still there was no reply.

It was no time for indecision. Bending over the girl, he saw that her eyes were open and he talked low to her for a minute. She understood, nodded, and sighed in relief.

Then he stepped through the window into her room, turned off the open cocks, and hurried into the hall.

He descended the stairway with a stealthy step and darted through her father's store, passing out of the door before Fong Toon, staring at him with amazed, wide-open eyes, could grasp an inkling of the situation.

Luk Chan went down the sidewalk at a rapid dog-trot, turned up Clay and into Waverly Place. He had gone about fifty yards along the narrow alley when three figures sprang out of the shadows behind him. Three revolvers barked and three spits of flame flashed in the darkness. He felt the "pi-i-ng" of a bullet as it whizzed past his cheek, another chipped a fragment of cloth from the shoulder of his blouse, and the third went wild. Miraculously he had escaped. But his shrift might be short.

He dived into an open doorway and bounded up the stairs, unlimbering his revolver as he fled. There were six shots in the "automatic" pistol and he would give a good account of himself before they got him. As he reached the second landing he heard the footfalls of his pursuers and their guttural exclamations. A head bobbed out of a doorway, but bobbed back again in affright when it saw the grim highbinder, revolver in hand.

He mounted to the third floor, and running to the end of the hallway, found a ladder that led to the roof. Quickly climbing it, he knocked off the scuttle cover, and when he had crawled through tried to pull the ladder after him. But it was stationary, so he jammed the cover back in place and ran across the graveled roofs, easily leaping the narrow spaces between the buildings. A cry told him that his enemies were close behind.

He paused at the edge of a coping and his heart missed a beat. There was a light-well between the two walls and it was at least ten feet to the farther one, which was a trifle lower than the roof on which he stood. He was panting from his exertions, and a miss meant instant death.

He could not retrace his steps nor run to the end of the well. His mind was made up quickly. Hurrying back a half-dozen paces, he drew a deep breath, then bounded forward, sprang on to the coping, and launched himself into space.

Fortune favored him and he struck the roof-edge, but stumbled and sprawled forward on his face. A bullet threw up the gravel close to his head, and he scrambled on hands and knees to the shelter of a brick chimney just beyond him. Dodging behind it, he took a pot-shot at his foremost pursuer and smiled grimly as the tong-man threw up his hands and tottered backward.

He waited, thankful for the breathing spell, but his enemies were wary, and though he peered cautiously around the chimney edge, he could see no further sign of them.

Then another fear possessed him. Perhaps they would descend to the street and enter the building he was hiding on. It was on a corner and he could not leap back across the opening. He would be caught. There was but one chance of escape. He must beat them to the street.

He crawled on his stomach, expecting momentarily to be shot, to a glass skylight in the center of the roof. It was fastened inside, but it was the work of an instant to break a pane with his revolver, and he shot the bolt. He threw it up, slid down the ladder, and fortunately found himself in a hall, at the head of a narrow stairway where a gas-jet was burning.

He leaped down the stairs, three at a time, and, after the second turning, landed at the street door. Hiding his pistol in his sleeve, he slipped out into the alley just in time to see the back of a police man, revolver in hand, whistle shrilling at lips, racing down Waverly Place while dozens of wildly excited Celestials dived through their doors, closing them and drawing their shades, fearful of flying bullets.

He walked slowly around the corner, pulled his hat over his eyes, and strode up Dupont street to California. Diving into the alley half-way down the block, he entered the joss-house back of Louie Toy's store. Here he might have time to think, to form some plan of escape from the vengeance of Ming Tai.

Lucero's warning had not been groundless.

The plot was carefully contrived. His life had been saved by a miracle. His confidence returned as he climbed the stairs,—but he held the shrewdness of his enemies too lightly. As he reached the first landing a slouching figure slipped into the doorway and stole after him on felt-shod, noiseless feet.

At the second floor he entered the swinging doors that led into the ceremonial room of the joss.

He crossed the polished floor and had traversed about two-thirds of the distance to the altar, when the door swung open again, a somber figure stood on the threshold, and leveled a revolver at his retreating back.

But the shot was never fired.

There was a light, swishing sound, a gleam of flashing metal, and the assassin pitched forward on his face. The handle of a stiletto protruded beneath his shoulder, and Juan Lucero, stepping out of the hallway, leaned over him and drew out the blade, wiping it nonchalantly on his unconscious victim's blouse.

Luk Chan, startled by the noise, turned, revolver in hand, and read the story of his escape in Lucero's attitude.

Slipping his knife into his girdle, the Mexican spoke: "I come in just the nick of time; *si*. I watch from the roof. I see the *malo hombre* follow queeck behind you. I run to the front. You come in the door. He come in, too. Then, *dio carno*! I rush down the stairs like I am mad. I get here just in time. What you think, *amigo?*"

"There is a blood-bond of friendship between us," muttered the tong-man fervently. "Luk Chan will not forget."

"No, no. Must not talk now. Must hide Chinese man. Then Luk Chan must hide too."

"No, I will go to the street. Others may follow."

"Please, please must not go. See *unos, dos,* half-dozen Chinese men and three, four policemen too, all on street. They look for some one. Must hide in here."

Luk Chan shrugged his shoulders, then stooped over and caught the limp body beneath its arms and dragged it to the end of the hall. Opening a little closet, he thrust it inside, and Lucero threw the hat and pistol after it.

"He not need hees gun now," he said drily, as the Chinaman closed the door. Then they hurried back to the altar-room.

At one side of it, running nearly ninety feet along its wall, was the great gilded Dragon used in ceremonial parades and at the celebration of the festivities of the Chinese New Year.

In the Portola procession, the year before, the Chinese division had been awarded the first prize, and its most spectacular feature had been the Dragon. Twenty Celestials had borne it on their shoulders, with only their slippered feet showing beneath its green-scaled, glittering sides. Two men inside the gigantic head had pranced a zig-zag course along the streets, and the lithe body had responded with serpentine undulations that were singularly effective.

A thought struck Juan Lucero as he looked at the Dragon. He hurried across the room and laid his hand against its head. It was at least eight feet high and nearly five feet in diameter, constructed of *papier mache*, and extremely light in consequence.

A red and curling tongue protruded through gleaming teeth. Great, staring eyeballs turned upward, and the creature seemed to grin at him,—a golden grin of fascinating hideousness.

He placed his fingers beneath its lower jaw and lifted it, turning it partly over on its side, while the green scales of the body crinkled rustlingly in response.

The shrill rattle of a police whistle was borne to them through an open window.

"Queeck," he commanded, and pointed to the opening.

With swift understanding, Luk Chan dropped to his knees and crawled inside the head.

Lucero let it fall back to its original position and stole silently from the room.

CHAPTER X

THE DRAGON'S HEAD

Detective Sergeant Bray, Officer Mulcahey, and a squad of policemen turned all the tong headquarters and every joss-house and Chinese gambling-den in San Francisco topsy-turvy in an attempt to get on the trail of the warring hatchet-men. But their efforts were fruitless. The wily Mongols that they questioned either could not "sabee," or professed ignorance. Though several arrests were made, not one of the suspects could be identified as an offending high binder. Several Hop Sing men and also several Bo Sing men were put through a form of the third degree at headquarters while the officers continued their search, but they were as inscrutable as their wooden joss.

Strange to say, Ming Tai, in a secret interview with Bray, did not mention Luk Chan's name. His enemy had disappeared from his usual haunts. The old fish dealer's hired murderers had reported to him. One of them was wounded and was secreted in a basement back of a clam-depot. They thought that a bullet had found lodging in the Bo Sing man's body, but they were not sure.

Ming had told the detective on a former occasion that Luk Chan belonged to the Hop Sings, and now he was between two fires; so he kept a still tongue beyond trying to convey the impression that the fight was the result of some private grudge, and not an affair of the tongs.

When they searched the joss-house the body of Lucero's victim was found huddled in the closet where Luk Chan had hidden him. A revolver lay by his side, but none of its chambers were empty, and when they dragged him out into the light they discovered the knife-thrust beneath his shoulder, but there was no evidence on which to hang a clue save the fact that he was recognized as a Hop Sing man.

While Bray and the two policemen were going through his clothes, Officer Mulcahey did a little investigating on his own account. The big Dragon, stretched snakily along the side of the room, fascinated him. He prodded its scaly sides with his club, lifted up an edge here and there, and peered beneath it. A fancy had struck him: perhaps some highbinder was hidden there, waiting an opportunity to get another victim, as he came to his devotions.

He gave it up at last and was about to turn away when the gilded head attracted him! He tapped it with his stick. There was a hollow sound, and he grunted. He might as well have one last look, then he would be satisfied.

He stooped and squinted through the half-open mouth, shading his eyes with both hands.

Suddenly he realized that two luminous orbs were burning back into his own with an ominous gleam.

He caught his breath and his lips opened to call out to his comrades when a sibilant phrase held him.

"My God, Luk Chan!" he muttered, and darted a swift glance in Bray's direction.

But the detective was busy with his search, and "Mul" pressed his lips close to the opening.

A whispered query, a quick answer, a muttered assent, and he straightened, joining his comrades, with the suggestion that they ring up the morgue and not "be wastin' no more time in these diggin's."

They left an officer in charge of the body, and within fifteen minutes the morgue wagon clattered up to the joss-house and the policeman and his "evidence" were taken away.

When the coast was clear Juan Lucero slunk into the entrance and darted up the stairs.

A hurried visit to the Dragon's head assured him of Luk Chan's safety, and they had a long conference. At last they came to an understanding and he left the building.

Just as he slipped through the door he saw Ming Tai, half-way down the block, headed in his direction. A thought struck him, and he smiled. Fumbling beneath his blouse, his fingers touched a familiar object. With a murmur of satisfaction, he drew back into the shadow, and as the old tong-man passed him he sprang out and thrust something into his palm.

Ming Tai leaped back, startled, and turned to stare at the fleeting form. A gust of wind caught the boy's hat and whisked it from his head. He recovered it quickly, but the damage was done. Ming had recognized him.

He was gone in an instant, and again horror seized the fish dealer as he gazed at the object in his hand. Again the little white disk. Again the tiger-cat. He had been frightened before, but this time terror struck him to the very marrow. His knees shook. He clutched his bosom and leaned against the wall. Slowly he recovered his faculties, but he did not regain his mental poise.

What did it mean?

He had thought all along that it was the warning of some tong enemy, but the peccant wind had thrown a new light on the subject.

The Hop Sing man, his tool, had been killed by a dagger thrust.

Ah! He had it now! The Mexican was the knife-thrower who had been concealed in Louie Toy's cellars. He had killed the hatchet-man. There were others implicated in the battle besides people of his own race.

He shivered. Would he be the next victim of Lucero's deadly skill?

In Louie Toy's cellars! In Louie Toy's cellars!!

By the sacred bones of his ancestors, he had it now! Yes, he had it now! He had solved the riddle.

What a fool he had been!

Louie Toy, masking as his friend, had been his enemy and was seeking to destroy him. The Mexican, in gratitude for Louie's protection, had become his tool. And they had used this method to unnerve him, to mislead him, to throw him off the track until they were ready to make an end of him. He was crafty; he knew the tong-men's ways; he had had an intimate acquaintance with barking pistols in the past, but had passed unscathed through more than one desperate battle. He must not permit himself to quail now.

But this silent whizzing messenger of destruction! There was no escape. The dead Hop Sing fighting man was sufficient evidence of that.

Even now he felt the shadow of death upon him and clutched at the wall. He had intended to visit the joss-house, but he changed his mind. His devotions could wait.

Louie Toy meant business. Louie had far more wisdom than he had given him credit for. And the Mexican was becoming bolder.

A fateful chip had been deposited in his till, another had come to light under the bean-jar's cover in his gambling-house, a third had been concealed in his hat, but this last one had been delivered in person. It could mean only one thing: Sen Chee's father was ready for action. His time was short. How crafty the merchant was. He had determined to rid himself of two undesirable sons-in-law and was playing him against the more dangerous one. His turn would come as soon as he had disposed of Luk Chan.

Action was imperative.

He must take the affair in his own hands; there was no one he could trust. Louie Toy must die before another day had gone. There must be no doubt of that.

Peering furtively about him, he hurled the poker chip into the street, turned down his hat brim, tucked his hands into sleeves crossed on his bosom, and hurried back to his store.

The joss-house was the scene of many curious comings and goings. It was deserted throughout the balance of the night, and the old Dragon guarded its tenant safely.

But the morning was still gray when Officer Mulcahey mounted the stairs. He had business with Luk Chan.

He lifted the head and the tong-man crawled out. They held a somewhat heated argument and at last the policeman gave in.

Sen Chee's lover handed him a package of bills. "There are five hundred dollars," he said. "It is more than you need, much more. Send some one you can trust to the steamship company's office, and see that your errand is done by noon. Visit me before you go on duty, and keep the balance as your reward. I think, under the conditions I can trust you. But the way must be clear."

Mulcahey looked at him for a moment, then stretched out his hand.

"Say, you're white, all right," he mumbled. "Leave it to me. I'll be on the job. I've got a pull with them people anyway."

Luk Chan's nostrils dilated, he hesitated, pride almost mastered him. Then he thought better of it and caught the proffered hand in a hasty grip.

San Francisco's Celestial quarter was draped in twilight when Juan Lucero helped a timid Chinese maid to climb the ladder that led, through a scuttle, to the joss-house roof. He waited by the opening, while she hurried forward to join a shadowy form that stood near the coping. Juan's fingers toyed with the pearl handle of a stiletto, and he smiled as he thought of his last glimpse of Ming Tai and the ashen pallor of his face.

Luk Chan drew Sen Chee to him, clasping both her hands in his and holding her close to his bosom as he looked into her dear, uplifted eyes.

He murmured low words of affection and she sighed in happiness, drooping her head upon his shoulder.

"Oh, my beloved, you have come back to me from the borders of the eternal vale. The lily blossom saved our lives,—yes, both our lives, Sen Chee,—for its scent called me to you."

"Both our lives, Luk Chan?"

"Yes; for my soul would have sought yours in the Vale of the Thousand Years."

"You do not mean—"

"Life would not be worth the living without you." He smiled. "And I would have cheated my enemies. There is a price upon my head. Ming Tai has planned to have me killed."

She started.

"Ming Tai! Then you know—"

"I know nothing save that he is my enemy and that I escaped his vengeance by a miracle."

She did not seem to hear. She was staring wide-eyed into vacancy. She thought of a conversation she had overheard one day from her balcony.

A tremor ran through her form and Luk Chan's arms tightened about her. But she pressed her hands against his bosom and thrust him away.

"But my father; my father!" she cried. "Surely you cannot love me when my father's hand is against you."

He misread her meaning.

"It was but natural. I am sorry that I had to strike, but it was the only way. He discovered us together on your balcony—"

"O—o—oh!" She threw herself into his arms and rested there content as he bent over her. An awful weight had been lifted. Luk Chan did not know that her father had plotted with Ming Tai. That last innocent answer of his was a portent of the future. Now she would do anything that he might ask of her. She would fly with him to the remotest corner of the earth, if he commanded it, and give up, for him, all living ties. He would not hate her now. He would never know that her father had planned his murder, and that, faltering between love and duty, she had risked her lover's life and held her tongue.

As if in answer to her thoughts, he spoke:

"Sen Chee, the time has come. If I would live, I must find safety in flight. Will you go with me wherever I may go? 'Wherever you go, I will go, Luk Chan,' you said, that scented night upon your balcony. You must choose between your father and Luk Chan. Look deep into your heart, little Lily Flower; your future hangs on but a single word. If you give yourself to me, you will never cross your father's threshold again. Will you trust your heart to my keeping? Will you come to me—now?"

She nestled closer to him, and bending over her, he read his answer and his happiness in her eyes.

He was silent for a time. The moment was too precious for words. But every instant held danger.

"I will hide you in the Dragon's head," he said at last. "The old Dragon has been a good friend to Luk Chan, and he will hold safe guard over Sen Chee till her lover comes for her. The time will not be long. You have lost your father, Lily Flower, but you will be the Dragon's Daughter to-night. Let us go to him."

When he had stowed her in her hiding-place, Luk Chan sent Lucero back to the roof, and left the joss-house.

He had a mission to perform.

His blood-oath must be fulfilled.

His conscience was sorely troubled.

He had registered a secret vow to kill Louie Toy. Sen Chee would never know. The news would be kept from her, and his duty to his tong would end. If he fled with clean hands he would be branded a coward, his memory would be reviled, his tong brothers would call down the curse of his ancestors upon him through the ages and his soul would never be purged of torment,— torment eternal.

His point of view seems monstrous.

But Luk Chan was a highbinder, a fighting tong-man, with all the traditions of his race, and to even the most peaceful Celestial the breaking of an oath is an unpardonable sin,—not oaths taken in the courts of the White Devils, meaningless words jumbled together and administered by bull-necked, bulldozing policemen who had no respect themselves for the sentences they mouthed, but oaths taken before their josses, with all the impressive rites of their religion. Such an oath could not be broken.

Louie Toy, with mandarin cap settled back on his head and a long strip of plaster on his temple, stood in the doorway of the Canton Bazaar, hands thrust in sleeves, puffing lazily at his pipe, outwardly content with the world, but nursing an inward turbulence.

Luk Chan slipped along the wall. His hand clutched the butt of a revolver held against his bosom beneath his loosened blouse. It would be but the work of a moment to whip it out, and then—!

He worked his way cautiously along the sidewalk. Nearly all the stores were closed by this time, and the street was deserted. He dodged from one doorway to another, and Louie Toy never once scented danger. Something attracted the merchant's attention, down the block, and with a desperate leap Luk Chan gained the shelter of the dark entrance next to the Canton Bazaar. He was not a dozen feet away from his victim and the rest would be easy.

He raised his revolver, sighted it, and his finger quivered on the trigger; but the image of Sen Chee dimmed his eyes. Strange! Her father's form was plain enough until he aimed the pistol, then he seemed to be pointing it directly at the body of his sweetheart.

He lowered the gun, thought of his blood-oath, and raised it again. But it was no use. He was aiming at the heart of Sen Chee. He was a coward! He drew back and hugged his dark corner for a while. At last he peered around the edge of the door; then,—then he saw Ming Tai slouching along the sidewalk, a bland smile on his face as he spied the merchant in front of his store. Two familiar figures rounded the corner a half a block in his rear.

Within ten paces of the bazaar, Ming's face suddenly changed, and whipping out a gun, he fired two shots in rapid succession.

Louie Toy crumpled up on his threshold and his assailant turned and ran—ran right into the arms of Detective Bray and Officer Mulcahey. He fought like a tiger, but they were too strong for him. Mulcahey twisted the smoking "automatic" pistol from his hand and in a jiffy a pair of handcuffs were snapped about his wrists.

"You'll swing for this, Ming," said Bray, gruffly. "We've got the goods on you."

Officer Mulcahey ran to the doorway, thrust aside Fong Toon and his squealing companions, and dropped to his knees by the side of Louie Toy. He turned him over on his back, tore open his blouse, and laid his ear close to his bosom.

A half-minute passed, then he rose.

"Dead as a mackerel," he said, slapping the dust from his knees.

Shortly after noon of the following day the *Korea* steamed majestically through the Golden Gate.

Unnoticed amongst the scores of Orientals in her steerage, a little Chinese maid clung timorously to the arm of a grim-visaged tong-man.

She murmured a low word and a glow of tenderness softened his eyes as he turned them on her.

Luk Chan and his Lily Flower were bound for the land of their ancestors,—the lotus land beyond the seas, where their heritage of love awaited them.

THE END